Doris's Decei
Book 4 in Clover Creek Community
Kirsten Osbourne

Copyright © 2023 by Kirsten Osbourne

Unlimited Dreams Publishing

All rights reserved.

Cover design by Erin Dameron Hill/ EDH Graphics

No part of this book may be reproduced in any form or by any electronic or mechanical means including information storage and retrieval systems, without permission in writing from the author. The only exception is by a reviewer, who may quote short excerpts in a review.

This book is a work of fiction. Names, characters, places, and incidents either are products of the author's imagination or are used fictitiously. Any resemblance to actual persons, living or dead, events, or locales is entirely coincidental.

Kirsten Osbourne

Visit my website at www.kirstenandmorganna.com

Chapter One

Doris stood between Melody and Mr. Jefferson, focusing all her attention on her wedding vows. She and Melody were having a double wedding ceremony that had been planned for all of ten minutes. She shook a little, not sure how comfortable she felt with Mr. Jefferson, whom she'd only known for an hour, but she was pretty certain she wasn't up to making the rest of the trip to Oregon City.

Mr. Jefferson had a farm in Clover Creek, Oregon Territory, and she was pleased to join his household rather than driving the rest of the way to Oregon City.

Shortly after she'd joined the company she had, one of the older sons of a friend had agreed to hitch her oxen for her every day and he'd also taken her shifts on the watch. Doris felt a bit badly for lying to everyone, but it had felt necessary when she'd joined with all the other wagons to go west on the Oregon Trail.

She repeated her vows when prompted, and she allowed Mr. Jefferson to kiss her cheek once they were pronounced man and wife. Now she only had to get the belongings she needed from her covered wagon, which would be mostly personal things.

Her mother had died in January, which had finally freed her to go west as an emigrant. For the longest time, she'd thought she'd spend the rest of her life doting on her mother, and caring for her in her sickness.

Doris had just barely finished school when her father died. Her mother had begged and begged her to stay with her and not find a man to marry. Now, thirty years later, she was past child-bearing age, and certainly past the age where she was marriageable—as a spinster anyway. But as a widow, the whole world had opened up for her, leaving her free to pursue her dreams.

Initially, she had hoped to get her piece of land and perhaps start a boarding house near Oregon City, but the Trail had been much harder for her than she'd dreamed it would be. Being introduced to a man who had recently lost his wife was what she'd needed to stop her journey west and marry a stranger.

Maybe her life would have been easier if she'd continued her journey, but she was definitely starting to believe the elephant didn't exist. Oregon City was so far away.

Doris smiled at her new husband. "Should we go and collect my things? Perhaps the lad who has been hitching and unhitching my wagon daily would like to take it with him."

Mr. Jefferson—Andrew, as she must remember to call him—nodded. "That would be good. Or we could leave it where it is and only take the things you desperately need. And the oxen, of course. I could add your oxen to my dairy farm."

"I brought only cows, so that would work well. I considered a bull, but they tend to be more obstinate and difficult to drive from what I've been told."

Andrew nodded. "Let's head out to your wagon and find what you need. I'm a farmer, and you know farmers need to be awake early for their morning chores."

"Yes, I'll say goodbye to our captain and meet you outside in five minutes."

At Andrew's nod, she headed toward where she'd last seen the captain, but he was nowhere to be found. The church was overcrowded with the people of Clover Creek, who had made their journey on the Oregon Trail the summer before, and her own company consisting of nineteen wagons and all the people that went with them.

Finally, she spotted the kind man on the other side of the church from where she stood. She hurried across the large room to him. "Thank you for being willing to take on a widow for the journey. I understand a lot of captains don't."

Mr. Stevens nodded, smiling at her. "I didn't see a need to keep women from going west alone when the government is happy to give you free land."

"I still thank you for it. The journey was made much easier by having a captain who wasn't grudging about my presence." She shook his hand. "And now I'll get what I need from my wagon. Please let everyone know they may take whatever they find."

"Thank you for your generosity."

Doris hurried out to meet Andrew, not wanting him to be upset with her this early in their marriage. He helped her onto the wagon seat, and they went to the camp, spotting her friend Melody doing the same with Mr. Appleby.

Doris needed a few things from her wagon. Most everything in it had been purchased for the journey. She did get the flour, sugar, and jerky she'd purchased that afternoon. And she took the small jewelry box her mother had left her and all the clothes she'd brought along.

Each thing was handed to Andrew as she found it, and finally, she climbed down from the back of the wagon. "Everything else can help the other families in my company," she said softly.

Andrew nodded, helping her back onto his wagon seat, even though he'd just watched her scramble into the back of her old wagon as if it was the easiest thing to do. "Now we'll have to get the cattle," she said. "I had each branded on the neck with my initials so they would be easy to tell from the others."

Andrew frowned. "Why don't I take you home so you can get settled, and I'll borrow my daughter's new brothers-in-law. They've offered to help several times as I've been building my house, so I'm certain they won't mind."

"That sounds like a good idea." She waited in the wagon as he returned to the church to ask for his needed help.

He came out shortly after with a young man who introduced himself as Jared Appleby. "I'm going to gather whoever I can, and we'll find the cattle while Mr. Jefferson takes you home. We'll see you in a little while."

Andrew climbed into the wagon beside her. "He and Roy are going to help and hopefully someone else. I don't know. He did tell me to go home and expect to have extra cows in the morning."

"Wonderful. That was much easier than it could have been."

Andrew nodded. "I think we all still have the mentality of the trail. We do what we can for others because we know we'll need them to return the favor in the future."

Doris nodded, smiling. "That's how my company was as well. I will miss the different women I was with in the evenings, but I will not miss that horrible journey."

"One of the ladies in our company called it a 'death march.' The description seems as apt as anything else," Andrew said.

"Did that woman make it?"

"Oh, yes. She's the midwife here. Her oldest daughter married along the trail, but Mrs. Mitchell simply continued along with her family. She complained a lot though."

"I wanted to complain a lot," Doris said. "But I couldn't figure out what that would help, so I stayed as positive as I could in my dealings with others on the trail."

He smiled. "I understand. I wanted to complain after my wife died. My daughter was a good little homemaker but married and moved away shortly after her mother died. No point in complaining about a thing, and I'm glad she's happy."

"Am I right that she married one of Mr. Appleby's sons?"

"Yes, she married his middle son, Sam. He's a good man, and he treats her very well."

"I'm glad." Doris looked out over the beautiful valley she would live in with him. "Do you ever have to go over Big Hill? Or is it just the once to get here."

Andrew smiled. "Just the once. Don't worry. I've done since we arrived, and I don't know if I ever would again. My daughter did fine coming down the hill, but my poor wife... shook for hours afterward. And you know how it is...we couldn't slow down because someone was afraid after coming down the hill. We had to keep going."

"There were many times we all needed a rest and kept going." Doris shook her head. "It's a very hard journey."

"Is that why you decided to marry? You didn't want to have to continue to Oregon City?"

She shrugged. "That was part of it. I had no idea the journey would be so taxing. Part of it is that I wanted to marry again." She turned from him and closed her eyes as she fibbed about having been married. "And part of it was that I wanted to begin my future sooner if that makes sense. I didn't feel the need to go all that way, open a boarding house, and then start living."

Andrew nodded. "I understand. I'm glad we finished the journey because I have free land for myself and my animals, but if I had thought I could start a farm without going all the way to Oregon City, I'd have done it in a heartbeat."

"Do you have favorite foods I could make for you?" she asked, changing the subject. She wasn't ready to tell him yet that she'd fibbed about having been married.

"I like just about everything. I know Fiona has a good kitchen garden this year. I don't know if she's willing to share her bounty, but if she is, it would help us a lot."

"I wish I'd been here in the spring to plant one of our own, but it just didn't happen. Do we have money to buy the vegetables we need?"

Andrew shrugged. "I do more trading than I do buying. I tend to keep whatever money I have for emergencies."

"Is there a bank in town?" she asked.

"No, the town was founded by our company, so it's not even a year old yet. But barter is a great way of doing things here. You'll find that most of the farmers and the store in town will barter for what they need." He shrugged. "I've eaten at the boarding house in town two meals a day since my daughter married. I trade the milk she needs for her daily cooking and baking for free meals. It works out well for both of us."

Doris nodded, thinking about the money she had stashed away. If she needed to use some so he could hold onto his, she wouldn't complain.

Finally, he pulled up in front of a small house. Though small, it looked like a very nice house to her. "I expected to be living in a cabin."

"We lived in one last winter, and my wife died of pneumonia. This year, we'll be warm." He helped her out of the wagon and led her inside, so she could see the house he'd worked so hard to build. "I moved in two weeks ago."

She went toward the kitchen first and found a real stove there. "You paid for a new stove, even though you didn't have a wife to cook for you?"

"I paid for it so my daughter could cook for me, but she married before it arrived."

Doris smiled. "Isn't that how life goes?"

"It does seem to be how my life goes." He shook his head. "Nelita would have been so proud to use that stove, and I couldn't get one here until after she passed."

"Nelita was your wife?" Doris asked.

Andrew nodded. "Yes, and she was a wonderful wife. I wish she could have had more children after Fiona, but we were a happy family."

"I'm sorry for your loss."

"I know you understand about loss. Knowing you had lost your husband made it easier to marry you. You'll have to tell me about him when you're ready."

Which would never be, Doris thought. How was she ever going to be able to admit she'd never been married when she'd made it very clear she was a widow? She'd figure it out, and it would need to be soon.

She opened one of the cabinets and exclaimed in delight. "These are wonderful. I'll be able to keep so much right here in the kitchen. Did you make these?"

Andrew shook his head. "That's one of the very few things I didn't make. A man in our company, who settled at the edge of town, made them for me. He's a furniture maker, so let me know if you see anything missing. We'll have him make it for us."

"So far, it looks like you thought of everything." She wandered to the dining room and then the parlor. "This house is so cozy. I just love it!"

He showed her both bedrooms. "This one was meant to be Fiona's, and when she announced she was marrying, I thought for a moment about making my bedroom larger, but then I thought it would be nice to have an extra room. Now it will be yours."

Doris nodded, thrilled. He wanted a platonic marriage until they got to know one another better. She was certain it was partly due to his grief, but it did make things easier for her. "It's perfect for me. Thank you."

"I'll go bring your trunk in," he said.

Doris kept looking around. There was no more to the house than what she'd seen, but she kept seeing new details. She would enjoy making his little house a home. There were no curtains on the windows and no tablecloth yet. She could use some yard goods to take care of that. She had some she'd brought with her, thinking she would use them at her boarding house.

Instead, she could make her new home as beautiful and cozy as possible without spending any money.

She returned to the kitchen to explore and see what food he had on hand, but there was very little. There was some jerky in one of the cabinets, and she had a feeling he ate that for lunch daily.

As soon as he brought her flour and sugar in, she would at least feel as if she had some things they needed. She would need to make some butter. Instead of trying to keep track of all the things to be done in her head, she found paper and pencil and got to work writing out a list of all the things she could do, and would need to do, to be able to cook in his kitchen.

The following morning would need to be a boarding house morning, she was afraid, but hopefully, by the end of the day, she would be able to cook. She had a lot of work ahead of her, but she had time to do it. It would be wonderful being Andrew's wife and not just some fake widow from the east.

Chapter Two

When Doris woke the following morning, she got dressed, made her bed, and picked up her list of things she needed to do. The first needed to be shopping at the local general store so she would have food to fix for Andrew.

When she walked out of her room, she saw Andrew was there waiting. "Cows are milked. Are you ready to go to the boarding house for breakfast?" he asked.

She nodded. "And this should be the last meal we have to eat there. I'll make sure to get what I need from the store today."

"I've got a credit at the store for milk. It's not a lot, but it should be enough. The owner's family appreciates fresh milk and cream delivered every other day."

"Do you do the deliveries yourself?"

He shrugged. "I do the in-town deliveries myself, but most of the milk goes to a local dairy, and they pick it up themselves. I don't think there's anyone outside of town that doesn't have their own cow."

"Are we taking milk with us this morning?" she asked.

He nodded. "We are. A full milk can for the boarding house and two large milk bottles for the store. If you can shop quickly, we can get all that done before heading home."

"Absolutely. I could start making butter and sell it as well."

"I'm sure Margaret at the boarding house would love that. Ask at the store if they'd like the same. It's always nice to have trades happening."

Doris realized then her husband was going to be hard to part from his money. It was a good thing she had some of her own.

He'd already loaded the milk onto the wagon, so it was just a matter of going. He handed her up, and they started the short journey into town. None of the houses were far from the others because they knew they needed their community to survive.

On the drive to town, he pointed out many things she'd been too tired to notice the night before. It was amazing how much energy she had after sleeping in a real bed for the first time in months.

When they reached the boarding house, he walked straight to a small table in one corner of the main room. Almost immediately, a woman who had to be at least seven months along came to the table. "Coffee?" she asked.

Doris nodded. "Yes, always coffee!"

"This is Margaret. She owns and runs the boarding house with the help of her husband, Jamie."

"It's good to meet you. Thanks for feeding us this morning."

"Mr. Jefferson more than makes up for the meals with the milk he trades. I hope there will still be trading happening."

Doris hadn't considered that. "I suppose there will be some. I'll probably cook most meals though."

Margaret nodded as she hurried off to bring their coffee.

"Were you planning to continue eating here two meals per day?" Doris asked Andrew.

He shrugged. "I hadn't really thought about it one way or the other. I suppose we can eat here when we want and at home when we want."

Doris was disappointed. "I think you're going to love my cooking."

"I certainly hope so," he said, grinning. "But Margaret's one of the best cooks in the whole valley. We can lean on her some as you get used to life here."

"That's not a terrible idea," she said softly. "I want to get a lot of sewing done in the next few days."

"I can plan to cook lunch every day."

He grinned. "I've been skipping lunch, so that would be wonderful. Why don't we keep eating breakfast and supper here as you settle in, and you can cook lunch for me. I have missed having a good midday meal."

Doris smiled. She would have an opportunity to cook for him after all. When Margaret returned to the table with their breakfast and coffee, Doris asked about butter. "You wouldn't be willing to trade for butter, would you?"

"Oh, yes, I most definitely would! My husband has been helping me with it, as my girls are too small, so he'd be very happy to not have to churn any more butter for the rest of his life."

"I'll start bringing butter then. Could you use a full ball every day? Or less than that?"

Margaret clapped her hands as she put down their plates of bacon and pancakes. "Oh, yes. A full ball a day would be perfect. I serve most meals with bread and butter, so it will save me a great deal of work."

"I'm happy to do it," Doris said with a smile. She'd always loved to churn butter, because she could churn with one hand while the other held a book. More than anything in the world, she loved to read. Hopefully, the butter would pay for an extra meal per day if they would still eat two meals a day there.

The food was delicious. "Oh, she is a good cook!" Doris said.

Andrew nodded. "I'm sure you are too. I'll look forward to lunches at home."

After breakfast, they headed to the store next door to the boarding house. "The town blacksmith and his wife run this. He found he didn't have quite enough work in such a small town, so he opened the store here so he could make a little more."

"Well, that's nice," she said. "Maybe they could use some butter as well."

Doris quickly shopped, choosing food to make for their lunches. There were pies there as well. "Who bakes the pies?" she asked.

The woman at the counter smiled, a baby cradled in one arm. "I do. I love to bake. We have enough bachelors in the area, I wish I had time to bake bread as well, but I simply don't."

Doris bit her lip. "I could do bread in trade for things I need."

"Oh, that would be wonderful. You married Mr. Jefferson last night, right?"

"I did. I'm Doris."

"It's so good to meet you, Doris. I'm Penelope Jensen."

"The blacksmith's wife?"

Penelope nodded. "That's right."

"Well, how many loaves of bread would you like and how often?"

Penelope thought for a moment. "Is six per day too many?"

Doris shook her head. "No, we'll eat two meals daily in town, so I'm trying to fill the rest of my time," she said. "I have some sewing to do in the next few days, but I don't know what to do with myself after that. You can only scrub a clean floor so often."

Penelope laughed. "Margaret is such a good cook. Herbert and I eat there more often than we should."

"Could you use butter as well?" Doris asked. If Andrew wanted to trade, that was great, but she would help in every way she could. She was not a woman used to sitting idle while others worked.

"Maybe a ball of butter per week. I don't like to sell things that are better if kept cold."

"I understand that perfectly. Could I bring a ball of butter every Monday? Would that work?"

Penelope nodded, smiling. "I think we're going to have a good business relationship. Welcome to our valley!"

"I've never even dreamed I could live in such a beautiful place!"

"You'll love it here. The people are just as wonderful as the land."

"I look forward to Sunday when I'll meet more people!"

Doris carefully chose what she would need for lunch for the next two days, and the items were put onto her account. Andrew already had dishes, pots, and pans. All they needed was food to put on and in them.

On the drive home, Doris talked about how much she'd enjoyed getting to know the young women of the valley. "Please tell me there are some ladies that are closer to my age, though."

Andrew smiled, nodding. "Yes, there are several ladies nearer to your age."

When he dropped her off, she immediately started her daily baking. As much as she loved cooking and baking, she was happy to have found an outlet for her talents. She wondered if she could also bake cakes for the store, but she didn't want to seem too greedy for money. Though she was certain they could easily make it on the trades Andrew had set up, it felt good not to be a burden on him.

She made a simple shepherd's pie for lunch, hoping it wouldn't be too heavy of a meal, because she knew he had to be out in the sun working yet. Thankfully, now that it was September, it was getting cooler during the day, and since she was no longer driving her wagon everywhere, it should be much easier to get things done.

When Andrew came in at noon for the meal, she served the shepherd's pie with a fresh loaf of bread. Other loaves were cooling around the kitchen.

Andrew smiled when he saw what she'd fixed. "That looks and smells delicious." He took a deep sniff. "You have no idea how much I've missed the smell of baking bread in my home."

"I love baking. There was no time to make a cake today, but there will be many cakes, pies, and cookies in our future."

"And I will have milk to go with all of it."

They had a light conversation as they ate their meal together. "I'm working on my winter pasture for the cows. A neighbor is trading corn for milk, and I'm thrilled for the trade. The corn will feed the cows all winter, nourishing them so they can make the milk he wants. Should I offer to add butter to our deal?"

"If you think he'd like that," she said. "I really do enjoy churning butter, even though my arms get tired from it."

"Is it asking too much to add it?" he asked, concerned. He had seen his wife hurt herself with all the chores around the house, and he didn't want to see the same thing with Doris.

"Not at all. The store only wants one ball of butter per week, so I'll be making one for us, one for Penelope, and seven for the boarding house. That's only nine per week. I did twenty-one per week at home."

"You made butter back east?"

Doris wished she hadn't said so much. "Yes, for a little extra income. It may take me a little while to build up those muscles in my arms again, but I don't think so. Not with all the driving I've been doing."

He nodded. "That drive was difficult. You were a widow when you left Independence?" he asked.

She nodded reluctantly. Perhaps keeping up the lie would be a problem. "I—" she started, ready to confess to the truth.

"I need to get back out there. I've dawdled too long. Thanks for the wonderful lunch, Doris." With that, he disappeared out the front door, and she sighed. She'd have to tell him another time. She simply worried that the longer she kept up the pretense, the harder it would be to admit to the truth.

She cleaned up their lunch dishes and took what was left of the shepherd's pie to the cellar. It would keep cool enough there they could have it again. Or if he had chickens, she could feed the food to them. She promised herself she'd ask that as they drove into town for supper.

The rest of her afternoon was spent churning butter. She wanted to be able to deliver the first ball to Margaret at suppertime. It would show she had every intention of keeping her word.

She made two balls that afternoon. One would last at least a week at home, and the other would go to Margaret at supper. She wrapped the bread in cloth to take to the store the following morning. She certainly hoped what she was doing would make her less of a burden on Andrew.

Doris found herself anticipating his return. She'd never spent so much time alone, except when she'd been driving on the trail, and most of that had been spent worrying about her future. It would be good to spend time with him when he returned from his day of work.

She found Andrew to be an attractive man. She hadn't really the night before when they'd married, but as she'd gotten to know what a good man he was, he'd gotten more and more attractive.

He came in from work shortly before five. "Are you ready?" he asked.

She nodded, taking the ball of butter she'd made for the boarding house. She had it in a small pot that had a lid over it. She wasn't certain how Margaret wanted her to provide it, but this would work the first time.

The entire drive to town, Andrew talked about his day, and she barely had a chance to get a word in edgewise, which was odd to her. He'd seemed like such a quiet man the night before.

Once they were at the boarding house, she gave Margaret the pot with the butter in it, and Margaret brought her back the pot a moment later. "Thank you so much. I'm so excited that I don't have to wear myself out churning butter anymore."

"In your condition, you should take a break from difficult tasks like that anyway."

"Oh, but I'm not going to take up the task again after the baby is born. You will be churning my butter for as long as I can convince you to do it."

Doris laughed. "I churned three balls of butter a day back home. And even with not churning more for a good long while, I found that the driving had kept my arms ready for churning."

"Good. I'm going to keep counting on you then." Margaret smiled, seemingly very pleased with the deal she'd made. "Coffee, milk, or water?" she asked.

"Milk," Doris answered immediately. She drank coffee in the mornings, but after noon, she had to switch if she wanted to get any sleep that night.

"All right. I'll be back in a minute."

Margaret brought the milk and put bowls of stew over rice in front of them. "Enjoy. And thanks again."

Doris took a bite and smiled. "She's a better cook than I am. I don't think I've ever said those words aloud before."

Andrew patted her hand. "You're a good cook too."

She stared at his hand where it covered hers for a moment. It was the first time he'd voluntarily touched her other than helping her in and out of the wagon. It felt odd, but right all at the same time. She was married, and her life was different.

Chapter Three

Sunday morning dawned, and Doris was awake to watch the sunrise. They would again go to the boarding house for breakfast, but afterward, they'd go to church. Doris couldn't wait for church because she would meet so many people in the community that she'd chosen to be part of.

She enjoyed the breakfast at the boarding house as always, and the church service afterward made her smile. Well, until the sermon started, anyway. The sermon was on honesty, and Doris felt as if Pastor Scott was looking straight into her soul, seeing her lies, and finding her lacking. The lie that had made so much sense to her when they'd started west seemed a huge burden now.

After the service, where she met what seemed to be every woman in the community, they made the short drive home. Once there, Doris reheated the food from the day before for lunch.

As they ate, she asked, "Do we have chickens?"

Andrew nodded. "We do. Only five of them right now, but they are growing quickly. Soon we'll have enough that we can process the pullets for food. Right now, I don't think that's possible yet, though."

"Makes sense. Do any of them lay yet?"

"No, but they should be in a few months according to Fiona."

"I met Fiona that first night, but only had a chance to speak with her briefly at church this morning." Doris wanted to get to know his only child. The little she'd seen of her was delightful.

"Oh, I talked to both her and Sam this morning. They plan to come over this afternoon. They are excited about Sadie's pups."

"Sadie?"

"My dog. She's going to have pups any day, and they want to see her and talk to her. They have announced they're getting at least one of the pups for the ranch, but they're hoping for two. I guess it depends on how many Sadie has."

"What kind of dog is Sadie?"

"She's a mutt, which is perfect here. She's great for helping me move the cattle from one area to the next. Hopefully, by next summer, we'll have farmhands around to help."

"I think that would be good. Will you provide housing for them?"

He shook his head. "No, we have a boarding house in town. They can stay at Margaret's and eat there. Then I don't have to worry about housing or food. It would be nice to have a foreman live in the cabin, though."

"Have you done anything to hire a foreman?"

He shook his head. "I'll start advertising for someone in the spring. Right now we're just keeping all cows and butchering the steers. Keeping our primary bull for breeding, but we don't need other males. They just need to be fattened up to be sold at market."

"When is the market?" she asked.

He shrugged. "Probably next summer. I have butchered a few steers already. We should have more than we can use by next summer, though."

"Do you share the meat?" Doris asked.

Andrew nodded. "I share with Fiona and her in-laws now. They bring me some of the game they kill and some of the yield from their kitchen gardens. I think that's a lot of the reason Fiona will be here today. She'll want to get to know you and drop off some of their vegetables from the garden."

"I look forward to getting to know her and Sam."

"Sam's a good husband to her. Initially, I was a bit worried, but he's made her very happy."

"That's good to know!" Doris said. "I want to meet Sadie as well."

"Sadie's been hiding in the barn most of her time lately. She's getting anxious about those puppies making an appearance."

Doris was washing the lunch dishes when Fiona came into the house. Without a word, Fiona took an apron hanging from a nail on the wall and put it on, immediately wiping the dishes that had already been washed.

"I'm sorry I wasn't able to get away yesterday," Fiona said. "Melody's feet are covered in bloody blisters. We helped her around the house instead of making it here to visit. I'm excited to get to know you."

"I feel the same."

"I brought plenty of vegetables from the garden. You'll want to put them up. If you need my help, just let me know."

Doris laughed. "I'm pretty self-sufficient. I'm selling butter and bread in town now for extra money."

Fiona shook her head, lowering her voice to a whisper. "Don't let Pa fool you. He has plenty of money hidden away. He just likes to be able to make more."

"Don't we all?" Doris asked. "I don't mind helping with household money. I only have him and me to care for, so I'll get bored quickly otherwise."

"Anything to help you alleviate boredom then!" Fiona yawned behind her hand. "Sorry. We've kept busy all summer with our garden. I planted strawberries, blueberries, raspberries, and blackberries. As they're all perennials, we didn't yield from them this year, but next summer and fall, we will be covered in berries."

"Wonderful! I do like to bake lots and lots of pies. I'm baking bread for the store and providing butter to the boarding house daily."

"Good for you! Are you doing it for trade or money?"

"Trade. Your pa thinks we should still eat two meals a day at the boarding house, so he's thrilled to build up as much in trade as he can."

"Do you not cook?" Fiona asked, her brows narrowing. She'd specifically asked the two women who had joined their community if they could cook.

"I do! But Margaret is better, and I can't deny that. I've always considered myself the best cook, but she is phenomenal."

Fiona nodded. "I can't argue with that, and I'm sure Pa is being stubborn about it as he is with everything else."

"Your pa is stubborn?" Doris asked. It was a side she had yet to see of her husband.

Laughing, Fiona said, "Just wait until you've been married for a little while. You'll see just how stubborn he is."

"I'll look forward to that," Doris said with a grin. "He tells me you want to see Sadie and make sure she's doing all right."

"Yes," Fiona said. "But I also wanted to bring you some of my harvest. We're hoping Sadie will have a good eight or nine pups so we can have two. Have you gotten to meet Sadie yet?"

Doris shook her head. "No, but your father said she was hiding in the barn as she waits for the babies to be born."

"That's where I'll go see her then. There's no reason to make her come to us." Fiona wiped the last dish and put it into the cabinet. "This house is beautiful. Pa did a wonderful job on it."

"He did," Doris agreed. "Did you ever get a chance to live here?"

Fiona shook her head. "No. He finished just a couple of weeks ago, and I was married in late spring."

For some reason, Doris liked knowing she was the only woman to have lived in the house. She knew it wouldn't truly matter one way or the other but being the first felt good. "Do you mind if I rearrange the kitchen to my liking?" Doris asked. She knew Fiona had set up the kitchen and most of the house. It would be rude to simply start changing things.

"Not at all. This is your home!" Fiona said. "My pa may live here, but it's never been a real home to me. I lived in the cabin for a while, but that never felt like home either."

They entered the parlor to join the men, and found them standing up, ready to go outside. "Are we looking at Sadie?" Fiona asked.

Andrew nodded. "Sure. We'll go see her." He led the way out to the barn with Sam beside him. Fiona and Doris were in the back.

They found Sadie in an empty stall in the barn, lying on her side amid the hay, ten small puppies wiggling as they tried to nurse. "Oh, they're beautiful," Doris exclaimed. She knew the puppies were at a premium but wanted to keep one for herself.

Doris dropped to her knees in the hay, aware that Fiona was beside her. "I want to keep them all!" Fiona said.

Andrew shook his head. "No, you're not keeping them all. But if all ten live, you can take two."

"Oh, thank you, Pa! We need them to help with the cattle. Bastian has already decided he wants one of them to live with him in the cabin once Jacob and Melody move into the house they're building."

"And where will the other one stay?" Doris asked.

"With me, of course." Fiona grabbed one of the squirming puppies and held it under her chin, snuggling it close. "There are so many colors!"

All the dogs had short hair, but one was white with black spots, another was pure black, and another was gray. "It was bound to be this way," Andrew said. "We know Sadie is a mixed breed dog, and we have no idea who the father of the puppies is." He reached down and lifted the gray one. "These look like they could be half-wolf, which wouldn't surprise me a bit."

When it was time to return to the house, Doris wanted to stay with the puppies, but she knew better. It would be best if she stayed with Fiona, getting to know the girl as much as possible.

Fiona returned to the kitchen and the basket of food she'd brought. "I have carrots, potatoes, peppers, pears, pumpkin, and squash. I also have a couple of cantaloupes if you eat them. Pa won't."

"Thank you so much!" Doris dug through the basket. "Cucumbers! I love to make pickles. I wonder how they'd go at the store."

"No point in doing pickles," Fiona said. "Penelope makes pickles and sells them as well as her pies."

"Well, I can still make some to share with you then, can't I?"

"Of course!" Fiona said. "Sam loves pickles."

"Dill or sweet?"

"Both. I think he'd eat pickles for every meal if he could get away with it."

When it was time to head into town for supper, Andrew asked if the other two wanted to go with them. "My treat."

Fiona shook her head. "No, I have plans for supper. Thanks for the visit." To Doris's surprise, Fiona hugged her. "I'm glad you married my pa," she said softly.

"I think I am, too," Doris replied.

Before they left, Doris retrieved the other butterball she had in the cellar, planning to take it to Margaret. She loved the idea of trading services almost as much as Andrew did. Of course, Andrew was tight-fisted, and she didn't tend to be, but she'd learn to do things the way her husband would like.

Margaret was serving roast beef and mashed potatoes, and the food was incredible. "You need to share some of your receipts with me," Doris said when the younger woman came to check on them halfway through the meal.

Margaret laughed. "I don't know about you, but when I cook, I add a little of this, and a little of that, until it tastes right. I don't have any real receipts."

Doris nodded. "I'm the same unless I'm baking. And sometimes I do things that way when I bake as well."

"I heard you're baking for the store. I wish you'd talked to me first. I sure would have let you bake bread for me."

Doris bit her lip, looking at Andrew, who nodded. "How many loaves would you need per day? I'm only baking six per day for the store."

Margaret's eyes narrowed. "Would ten be too many?" she asked.

"Not at all. Why don't I bring one loaf tomorrow so you can make sure you're happy with it, and then I'll start doing ten per day for you."

"I'd need them here by six in the morning every day..."

"That would be fine. I can mix the dough the night before and let it rise in the cellar overnight. It always takes longer when it's cooler. Then I just have to be up by four to bake it. Andrew is up that early for milking anyway."

Margaret nodded, looking relieved. "This far into my pregnancy, everything I do seems almost impossible," she said. "I was never this big with the girls."

"I'll help in any way I can. I love to bake, and if we're eating here in town twice a day, it'll be nice to contribute to the meals we eat."

"And it will help me so much. I'll look forward to tasting your first loaf tomorrow, and if it goes well, I'll expect ten loaves on Tuesday."

"Sounds wonderful."

As Margaret walked away, Andrew smiled. "We don't need that much extra."

Doris shrugged. "I won't feel like I'm a burden on you if I can keep busy with cooking."

Andrew gave her a look that surprised her. She wasn't exactly sure what it meant, but it seemed to be...well...interested in her womanly attributes. In all her life, she'd never received a look like that from a man.

She took a deep breath, deciding to tell him her secret on the way home. He needed to know the truth before he developed feelings for her.

Andrew was particularly chatty on the way home, telling her how excited he was that she was fitting in so well. "Fiona already seems attached to you. I'm surprised to see her feel something quickly because she was close to her mother."

"I want to be close to Fiona. She'll be the mother of our grandchildren." Doris had always regretted not having children, and the idea of grandchildren made her heart flutter just a little. "I need..."

"Anything you need you can get from the store in the morning. Will you get up early tomorrow to bake the bread?" he asked.

"I will. But I need to tell you..."

"You don't have to tell me anything," he said. "I'm so pleased with you, I just can't express it. You're exactly what I needed in a wife. And your cooking is wonderful."

"Just not as good as Margaret's?" Doris asked.

"No one cooks quite as well as Margaret does. That woman must have been born with an iron skillet growing out of her hand."

Doris laughed. Obviously, this wasn't the right time to explain her deceit to him. But she had to tell him soon.

Chapter Four

After Andrew and Doris returned home after supper, he asked if she had time for a walk or if she needed to get to work doing the things, she'd promised to have done the following day.

"I must get the dough mixed and divided for bread tomorrow. I wish I had time for a walk."

"Work needs to come first," he said, believing his words. "I need to milk the cows anyway."

While Andrew milked, Doris mixed up a huge batch of bread to take it to the store in the morning and also provide a sample for Margaret. She didn't doubt Margaret would want to use her bread because she had been making bread most of her life.

She carried the individual loaf pans downstairs once the dough was ready to rise and portioned out. She only had ten pans total, but it would be easy enough to buy a few more the following day. Knowing she'd get her money back on them made it a good idea to buy them.

She was waiting in the parlor when Andrew came back inside, hoping he would listen to her about her deception. She had never intended to deceive Andrew, just the wagon train, and only then because it had felt necessary. Surely her new husband would be able to understand her reasons for telling the biggest fib of her life.

Andrew took one step into the parlor and frowned. "I'm sorry, but I'm too tired to stay awake. Do you mind if I just go to sleep?" he asked.

"Of course not. I need to be up early in the morning, so we'll simply go to bed." Doris stood and walked toward him, meaning to go past him and head to her bed. She was surprised when he reached out and caught her shoulders, brushing a soft kiss against her lips.

She was even more astonished at how much she enjoyed the kiss. She'd never had a beau or a man who had dared try to kiss her, so this kiss from her husband after over forty years of being alone, simply felt right.

Wrapping her arms around him, she gave into the feelings she was developing for Andrew. When he finally raised his head, she could still feel the kiss all the way down to her toes. Never would she have guessed that a man could make her feel so many things all at once.

"Goodnight, Doris," Andrew said softly as he went to his room.

Doris went to her own, knowing she had to be up early, but after that kiss, she spent too much time staring up at the ceiling and imagining a real marriage with a man who loved her. She certainly hoped it could happen.

Early the following morning, Andrew knocked on her door on his way to milk. "Time to get up and bake," he said.

Doris groaned and sat up in bed. "I'll be out in a minute or two." She had never been particularly fond of mornings, and now having to wake before the sun was even thinking of rising...well, it felt like too much.

When she was dressed, she left her room, going straight to the stove to start the fire within it. Then she went down the stairs into the cellar to fetch the loaves of bread she had rising. She'd done ten total, knowing she and Andrew would need some with the lunch she served...whatever that happened to be.

She took the large basket Fiona had brought produce in and filled it with the loaves of bread, each of them wrapped in a piece of cloth. She would need to churn butter that afternoon and a lot of it. Doris hoped she hadn't bitten off more than she could chew with all the extra baking she was doing, but she had a feeling that the work would keep her happy. She didn't need her mind to be idle or her hands either.

Andrew came inside with their milk for the day and set it on the counter. "I already have Margaret's milk in the wagon. Are you about ready?"

Doris nodded, feeling embarrassed to be with him this morning, after their kiss of the night before. Though she looked forward to a real marriage with him, she wasn't sure she'd make it through the embarrassment to get to that point.

She hefted the basket with all the bread, and Andrew immediately took it from her. "You don't need to carry such heavy things," he said.

"I suppose I don't." No one had ever been so kind as to carry things for her. A few men on the trail had done their best to make her work easier, but for the most part, it had only been her and her mother for her entire life.

She followed him out to the wagon, closing the door behind them, and waited until he'd settled the bread in the back, so he could help her up. He'd gotten into the habit of treating his first wife well, and she was thrilled he was treating her the same way.

As they drove, he talked about Sadie's puppies and how they ate well. "We'll keep one," he said. "You'll get your pick of the litter. Also, let's save any table scraps for Sadie while she's nursing them."

"I get to keep a puppy?" she asked. Her life hadn't been bleak but hadn't been filled with little privileges either. To her, owning a dog was a true privilege and one she was excited about.

"If you wanted to you could keep them all, but I've promised most of them to people in town."

"Ten would be a few too many. I'd love to keep one though. Can it be inside as well as outside?" she asked.

"Of course. Whatever you like. Just know that puppies are sometimes hard to housetrain."

"That won't bother me at all," she said.

She practically danced into the boarding house, giving Margaret the loaf of bread she'd brought. She had always put a bit of butter on the top of the bread before baking, making the bread so much better.

Margaret brought them coffee before carrying the bread into the kitchen to try it for herself.

When she brought their breakfast out, she had a huge smile. "If you can handle ten loaves daily, I would be grateful."

"Oh, of course. I'm thrilled to do it." Doris couldn't believe how pleased she was that she could help this woman, whom she'd known for just a few days.

"Thank you so much! I don't know what I did before you came here."

"Exactly what you had to do," Doris said with a smile.

"My husband said to thank you for him. He's thrilled not to have to churn butter after farming all day."

"Who minds your children while you work?" Doris asked.

"Oh, they play in the kitchen. I have a table in there and I put down different things for them to do while I work. Since I only do two meals per day, they only have four hours to stay entertained, and I'm right there if they need me."

"That sounds like a good solution to me."

"It works well. My daughters are very well behaved." Margaret hurried off to fill someone's coffee cup and Doris shook her head.

"She does so much for so many. I can't help but admire her."

"She told me she's always loved to cook," Andrew said. "She was very happy to trade milk for meals, and now bread and butter for meals. I'm glad we don't have to pay extra for you to eat here."

While they ate the French toast Margaret had made, Doris's mind was again on trying to decide what to do about the lie Andrew still believed. It was time she told him, but the boarding house was not the place to do it.

"Are you just dropping off bread today, or do you need something else?" he asked.

"I need to buy a few more bread pans. I'll be making as many as twenty loaves of bread per day, and I would like to not have to use the same pan over and over."

He nodded. "That would be good. You should get some meat for lunch there as well. I do enjoy our quiet lunches at home."

"So do I," Doris replied, truly enjoying everything about her marriage to this man. "Would you mind if we had something simple like bacon sandwiches for lunch?"

"Not at all. I like my bacon extra crisp."

"As far as I'm concerned it's not edible any other way," she said with a grin.

At the store, she quickly found what she was looking for, and she even found two little crocks to carry butter to the restaurant in. They would be perfect for the job, and she wouldn't have to constantly use her small pot for butter.

When she talked to Penelope, the other woman was thrilled to have the bread. "I'll let you know if this is enough. I've never sold bread."

"I can easily make more if you need it," Doris said, thinking of the extra time she would be kneading bread, but it would help her to not feel like a burden. For the first time in her life, she felt as if she was doing all she could to be productive.

"Thank you. I'll take you up on that once I determine how much we'll need."

Andrew came in then with two large milk jugs. "Let me know if you need more."

Penelope smiled. "I will. I can't believe how much milk I'm drinking right now. Herbert keeps laughing at me, but I don't mind even a little."

"I'll have your butter this evening when we come in for supper," Doris said.

"Wonderful! Thank you both!"

Doris left the store with food for their meals for the next couple of days and all the bread pans she needed. It would be exciting to learn how quickly her loaves of bread were sold.

On the drive home, Andrew told her what he would be doing for the day, and she was again unable to tell him about her lie. She wanted to get it off her chest, but he always talked about something else.

She was surprised when he kissed her as he left for the day, but his kisses were getting increasingly familiar, and she was feeling more and more comfortable with them.

Instead of starting on the chores she needed to do immediately, she went out to check on the puppies. Sadie kept looking at her as if she thought Doris could help her. Doris stroked the dog's head and ears, talking to her softly. "You're a good mama, Sadie. We're going to keep one of your puppies so you can always be together. Won't that be nice?"

After playing with the puppies, she went inside, made the beds and washed the bread pans from that morning. Then she pulled out the butter churn and went to work on the butter. She wanted two balls done before supper, and that would take around an hour. But there were so many other things she wanted to do as well.

She made Andrew three bacon sandwiches but only one for herself. She knew he was doing much harder work than she was.

As they ate their lunch, he talked about how much he enjoyed her company, and how happy he was that she'd agreed to marry him. Doris smiled and told him the same thing, but in the back of her mind, she couldn't help but wonder if he was going to hate her when she told him the truth about herself. What had seemed like a wonderful idea in Independence, now felt like a curse.

She had to tell him before bed that night, no matter how difficult it was to get him to listen to her.

The rest of her day was spent churning butter and putting up some of the vegetables Fiona had brought the previous day. She hoped there would be fresh game soon as well, so she could have it ready for the winter. She knew the store wouldn't be able to keep fresh meat for long.

The house was spotless when Andrew came in from milking that afternoon. Doris was thrilled with how much work Fiona had done to keep it tidy. She could already see that it had been plenty of work for the girl, because Andrew wasn't in the habit of picking up after himself.

He glanced at her when he walked in. "I'm hungry. Are you ready to go to town?"

She nodded, getting the two balls of butter and carrying them to the door, where he took them from her. "You should just ask me to carry heavy things," he said softly.

"The butter isn't all that heavy," she replied.

"It is too heavy for a lady to carry on her own, and that's that."

Doris nodded. "All right. I'll ask next time."

"Thank you," Andrew said, leaning down and kissing her cheek. "Let's get this butter to town. We need to be there before the store closes at five."

"I'm ready," she told him. And she was sure she was. Ready to go to town, but even more than that, she was ready to tell him the truth about herself. It was going to happen before bed, or she would lose her mind.

She delivered the butter to the store and then to Margaret, who brought them milk without being asked. "Pork chops tonight," she said. "I'm going to send Jamie out for some deer tomorrow. I would love some venison stew."

Doris smiled, nodding. "I love venison stew, and I haven't had it since I was a little girl. After my father died, there was no more venison."

Margaret frowned. "I even made it on the trail. I'll give you an extra large portion."

The pork chops and baked potatoes that were for supper that night were delicious. Doris had never loved pork chops, but whatever Margaret had used to season them was wonderful.

"Do you have any pigs?" Doris asked as she dug into her plate of food.

Andrew shook his head. "Not yet. I may get some in a few years, though. I need to ensure the dairy farm is established and ready to support us first."

Doris couldn't help but smile. The man was so careful with his money and his future. She was happy to help in every way she possibly could. If he kept her around after he heard about her lie.

Chapter Five

On the drive home from Clover Creek, Andrew once again talked about his day and his dreams for his dairy farm. Doris knew she had to start mixing the bread dough as soon as she got home, and she truly hoped she could talk to him about her lie first.

She listened, nodding, and finally, when he started talking about his hopes to have pigs on the farm within the next five years, she knew it was time to cut into the mostly one-sided conversation. "Andrew, I need to tell you something."

Andrew became quiet, seeming to be shocked that she'd said that. "What about?"

"When I met you, I was introduced as a widow. I let the company think of me as a widow because I thought I would have less unwanted attention from men on the trail if I was a widow."

"Are you saying you're married?" he asked, looking appalled.

"Well, I am married, but I'm married to you. The truth is, I've spent the last twenty years taking care of my mother, who was sickly her entire life. She died less than a year ago, and that's when I started planning my journey west. I've never married. I've never even had a beau."

"Why didn't you tell me before? Before we married?"

"I was afraid to that first night. I didn't want anyone from the company I was with to hear, and then they'd all think less of me for lying. Then we married, and I've been trying to tell you since, but...well, it's been hard. You talk about your goals and our future, and I love to listen. But I haven't had much chance to tell you anything."

"I see." Andrew wasn't sure how he felt about her never having married. "And you're telling me now for what reason?"

"Because I have no desire to have lies between us. I'm developing feelings for you very quickly, and I don't want my deceit to be a wall between us and our eventual happiness."

Andrew nodded as he stared straight ahead, driving home in full sunlight because it got dark late in the day where they lived. "Let me think on it. I'm not going to reject you because you presented yourself as a widow, but I need to think about how I feel about it. Lying is a sin, and you've been lying to me since before we married. It may be hard for me to trust you again."

"I can understand that. Thank you for not immediately rejecting me."

The worst part of it for Andrew was knowing he was now married to a virgin. A widow would be easier to make love with the first time. But a woman in her forties who was still a virgin? That was something else altogether.

He was silent for the rest of the drive home, and Doris felt more and more nervous about what his reaction would be. Perhaps he would think it was all fine, and not be upset at all, but there was a good chance he would find his way to anger.

She hurried into the house, not waiting for him to help her down from the wagon and started to work immediately on the bread she needed to make for the following day. As she dug her fingers into the dough, she tried to not think about Andrew at all, but that was impossible.

He was disappointed in her. She'd seen it on his face. She only hoped the two of them could get past her fib and become a true married couple, with love and intimacy.

She heard Andrew enter the house, but then she heard his bedroom door close. He wouldn't talk to her again tonight, and there would be no goodnight kisses.

Tears streamed down her face as she divided the dough and put it into individual pans. She only hoped they wouldn't have a marriage of convenience for long, because she was already in love with Andrew. That had to count for something, didn't it?

Andrew was very quiet for most of the week. He would talk when she spoke first, but simply to answer questions. He was still mulling over what she'd told him, and trying to decide how he felt about it.

By Saturday, Doris was told the store needed ten loaves of bread per day. Since she wanted a loaf a day for her and Andrew, she bought one more bread pan, but their credit at the store was growing daily. It felt good to contribute, even as she waited to talk to Andrew about what she'd told him.

On Sunday afternoon, Fiona and Sam came to visit again, and even Fiona noticed that there was something wrong between her father and his new wife.

"Why is Pa acting so strange?" she asked. "He seemed so happy the last time we were here, but now he doesn't seem to want to talk to you at all."

Doris frowned. "Let it be."

"You know what's wrong?" Fiona pushed.

"I do, and I beg you to just let it be. We'll work it out on our own."

Fiona frowned. "All right. I just wish I could help in some way."

"I appreciate that," Doris said. She wiped her hands dry on her apron after washing the last dish. "I have scraps to take to Sadie. I've been cooking a little extra every day so I could give her more food."

"I think that's wonderful." Fiona smiled at her stepmother. "I went to the store yesterday, and they asked if I wanted to use any of your credit, because you were building it up faster than you could spend it."

Doris laughed at that. "I'm just doing what I can to help your father with the finances."

"Which is great, but Pa doesn't need help."

"Anything could happen," Doris said softly. "Having money set aside will only help us."

"I guess," Fiona said. "Let's go see the puppies! Pa said you get first pick. Have you chosen a favorite yet?"

"I think I want the little gray one," Doris said, surprised that Andrew remembered his promise.

"He's a sweetheart," Fiona agreed. Walking into the parlor, she said, "We're going to see the puppies."

Sam got to his feet. "Not without me you're not."

As they walked to the barn, Doris hoped she would be able to get Andrew to speak with her soon. They had to be able to talk through what she'd told him. It had already been six days. Exactly how long did the man need to think about how he felt about her never having been married? It made no sense that he was so quiet about it.

In the barn, Sadie was excited to get the food, stood up, and the puppies fell off her. While she went to eat, they looked at the puppies, and Doris said, "I want the gray one. I don't have a name for him yet, but he's mine."

Andrew nodded. "We'll come up with a name." He said nothing else, though, and Doris was certain he was simply going to stop talking to her at all soon. She'd really messed up by not telling him the truth sooner. She should have just told him she had something important to say instead of waiting as long as she had.

The other couple went to supper with them that evening, and they had a wonderful meal of ham, creamed potatoes, and corn. "This is delicious as always," Doris told Margaret.

Margaret smiled. "I do my best."

Fiona and Sam had driven their own wagon to the boarding house, so Doris and Andrew were alone on the way home. As soon as they were out of earshot of his daughter and her husband, Andrew asked, "Did you tell Fiona why we're not getting along?" he asked. "She asked me, and I told her to mind her own business."

"I told her to let it be. It's not any of her business why we're having trouble, and I wouldn't try to sway her opinion."

"Thank you for that," Andrew said. "I don't want my daughter in the middle of it."

"I don't want her there either. But I wish I knew where I stood. It's been six days since I talked to you, and you haven't said much to me since then."

He sighed. "I'm still really trying to decide how I feel. I don't like that you thought you needed to lie, but I think I can understand why. I just wish you'd told me sooner...like the night we were married. It makes it hard to trust you now."

Doris nodded. "I understand." She wished it wasn't so, but she did understand. "So where do we go from here?"

"I'm not certain yet. I'm not going to get our marriage annulled or get a divorce. But I thought we were taking our time and having feelings for one another grow, and that couldn't be the case if you weren't being honest with me."

Doris bit her lip, deciding to put it all on the line. "I do have feelings for you, Andrew. They've grown a little more each day. I know you can't completely trust me now, but I hope you'll be able to in the future, because I would like for us to have a real marriage."

He looked over at her for a moment before nodding. "I'd like that too. I think."

"I know it's hard to deal with, but you need to let me know how you feel and what you want to do about it."

"All right." He pulled the wagon into the yard and jumped down, going around to help her down. "I'm going to put the horses up for the night and milk the cows."

"Does it matter that you always seem to milk them later in the day on Sundays?" she asked.

He shook his head. "Doesn't seem to."

Doris went inside to get the dough prepped for the morning's baking. Perhaps she and Andrew could spend a few minutes together after they were both finished with the chores at hand.

When she climbed the cellar stairs and walked to the parlor, he was sitting there, staring off into space. Usually, he read or whittled, but that day, well, he had too much on his mind, and Doris knew it was because of her.

She went into the parlor and sat beside him on the sofa, putting her hand over his on his knee. "I'm very sorry I didn't tell you sooner, and I hope that someday you'll be able to forgive me and trust me again."

He looked at her, his brows furrowed. "I have already forgiven you," he said softly. "The trust is what's going to be hard to come by."

"What can I do to prove I won't lie to you again?" She wanted to point out that she'd never really lied to him. No, it had been a lie carried over from when she hadn't been able to trust the company she'd joined.

"I don't think there is anything. We'll just have to muddle through and see how things go."

She sighed deeply. "I wish I had answers."

"I do as well, but it is what it is."

She decided to go out on a limb and say something he wouldn't expect. "I miss your kisses," she said softly.

He stared at her for a moment, slowly lowering his head and brushing his lips across hers. Then his hands went to her waist and he pulled her closer, deepening the kiss.

Soon, the kiss was more than she'd ever experienced before, but instead of wanting him to stop, she wanted to see where the kiss would lead. It seemed odd that they would make love when she was obviously too old for childbearing, but perhaps they could do it because they cared for one another. She didn't know if that was done, but she wouldn't object to seeing for herself.

Andrew pulled her onto his lap and moved his hands to cup her breast, never breaking the kiss. Doris felt things she'd never imagined she would feel, including a tingling in her stomach and an ache between her thighs. Maybe she couldn't have children, but she was enjoying this too much to stop.

Andrew lifted his head and looked into her eyes. "If you're going to tell me to stop, you need to tell me now. Otherwise, I'm taking you to my bed, and making you my wife in every way."

Doris looked deeply into his blue eyes. "Please don't stop."

Andrew didn't have to be told twice. He pushed her onto the couch beside him and then took her hand, pulling her toward his bedroom. Within moments, he had them both completely naked, and he was pushing her down onto the bed.

He continued kissing her instead of climbing atop her immediately as she'd expected him to do. His hands were all over her body, even at the ache in an area no man had ever touched.

When he moved one finger inside her, she let out a gasp of shock, that quickly turned to pleasure. She clenched herself around his finger, enjoying the feel of it inside her.

When he covered her with his body and joined them as one, Doris wrapped her arms around him and held on for dear life. His movements inside her were more than she'd ever expected.

Soon he'd finished and rolled to her side, leaving her wanting...something. It had felt good, but it wasn't quite enough.

He seemed to know though, because as soon as he caught his breath again, there was a finger inside her that was quickly joined by another. His hand made her feel so much, and she gasped, clasping him tightly inside her.

He held her close as she found her release, and he kept her close even as he was falling asleep. Doris hadn't expected to feel so much with him. She'd thought he'd find pleasure in her arms, but it had never occurred to her that a woman could find pleasure in a man's arms.

She settled down close to him, her head on his shoulder. She could get used to being a wife if it meant feeling as she felt at that moment.

The only thing that kept her from complete happiness was she didn't know if he'd ever trust her again. She wanted him to, but she'd made a mistake, and she would have to continue to wait as she found out whether or not he believed that she could be trusted.

She closed her eyes and sighed contentedly. Even if he never trusted her, if they could just keep things as they were, she would have a good marriage. Hopefully, he would learn that she was not the type of person who lied easily, but if he didn't, she was determined to be happy with him anyway.

Chapter Six

Doris was awake early the following morning to bake bread and get ready for the morning ahead. It seemed strange, leaving Andrew asleep in bed, but she knew it was important than she fulfill her obligations.

Andrew and Margaret had spoken and they'd decided that the Jeffersons could eat free two meals per day in trade, and they would also accrue two extra meals per week for whomever they wanted to eat with.

As Doris popped loaves of bread into the oven, she couldn't help but let her mind drift to the previous night's events and the pleasure she'd received in Andrew's bed. No one had ever told her that a woman received pleasure from a man. She'd been led to believe that only the men would receive pleasure from the marital act.

She worked on churning more butter while the bread baked because it was a mindless activity that allowed her to continue daydreaming. When she heard Andrew go outside to milk the cows, she wondered how he was feeling. Hopefully he was as pleased as she was that their relationship had become physical.

It took him as long to milk the cows as it did for her to bake all the loaves of bread they needed for the store and the boarding house. Carrying them in the same basket she had been, she wrapped each in cloth to get ready to go.

When Andrew came inside, he looked at a bottle she'd filled with something. "What's that?" he asked. He was used to her taking bread and even butter, but she had a bottle of a strange milky substance.

"Butter milk," she replied. "I think it may help Margaret. If not, I'll put it out for the pups."

"Sounds fine." He said nothing else as he carried the bread to the wagon for her, putting it into the back before helping her into the wagon.

"Do you regret what happened last night?" Doris asked as they started toward town.

Andrew shook his head. "No, I enjoyed it too much to regret it, and you are my wife. But I hope it doesn't make you think I can trust you fully, because I'm still not certain that's true."

"I understand," she said softly, though she wished things were different. With everything inside her, she wished she had the answer to what she could do to get him to trust her, but she decided it would just take time.

He carried the basket of bread into the back door of the boarding house with Doris right behind him. "Do you have any use for buttermilk?" Doris asked. "We don't really use it, and I thought it might be helpful for you."

Margaret nodded. "Yes! I would like the buttermilk for my own purposes. Both girls and I love to drink it."

"Then I'll bring it every day. It's better than wasting it." Doris hoped that Andrew wouldn't try to get Margaret to trade something for it. She wanted this to be a gesture of friendship toward the younger woman.

"I would appreciate that."

Andrew said nothing as they entered the dining room and sat down at the little table in the corner always reserved for them. "Will it be more work for you to bring Margaret the buttermilk?"

Doris shook her head. "Not really. I'll just have to keep up with a couple of milk bottles and keep them clean. There's nothing else involved."

"Good. I would like for the buttermilk to just be something between the two of you. I don't feel the need to trade or charge her for it."

"I was hoping that would be the case. I feel like Margaret was my first true friend here, and I wanted her to have something from me."

A slight smile curved Andrew's lip. "I'm glad we're thinking alike."

"It's nice isn't it?" Never had she dreamed she would marry a man who thought so much like her. It felt as if she'd walked into her own version of paradise. If only he could trust her then everything would be perfect.

At his nod, she grinned. "I think I'm going to spend the day working on curtains. I've delivered the butter needed for the Jensens, and Margaret is good. I can churn more in the morning while the bread is baking. I hadn't really realized how easy it would be to churn while baking. I feel like I've been wasting time my entire life."

"That sounds fine," he said.

"Is there anything around the farm you need my help with before I start on the curtains?" She said a silent prayer that he would ask her to go with him and work with him that day.

"No, nothing I need help with. Make your curtains."

Doris was a little sad he didn't want or need her with him, but Fiona had brought more vegetables that had to be put up. There was plenty of time to do the things she had to accomplish, and she would put her heart and soul into doing it.

When they arrived home, she made a simple meal for lunch, not thinking he much cared what he ate for the noon meal. She had it on the table when he arrived home after working all morning, and they ate mostly in silence.

She had just finished the lunch dishes when someone pulled up in the yard. Looking out the window, she saw it was Fiona.

Doris wiped her hands on her apron and went to the door. "Hello!" she called.

Fiona jumped down from the wagon. "I'm working on harvesting pumpkins and squash today. I know Pa doesn't eat squash but he loves pumpkin pie. I thought you might like to come and help me harvest. Emma is spending a quiet day with Henri."

Doris remembered the names Emma and Henri as Fiona's sisters-in-law. "I'd love to!"

"Jump in and let's go then." Fiona didn't bother to get down from the wagon seat.

"Should I bring a basket to harvest into?"

"No need. I have plenty." Fiona grinned as Doris scrambled up beside her. "Ma and I made lots of baskets last winter. We knew it would help us for the harvest this year."

"What a wonderful idea. Is that where all the baskets in the cellar came from? I feel like every time I turn around down there, I bump into another basket," Doris said, wondering about Fiona's mother. Perhaps Fiona would tell her about her if she wasn't too intrusive.

The drive to Fiona's home was short, and Doris looked all around her. She was a little surprised when Melody joined them. "I wasn't sure how much I'd see you outside of church," she said to the woman who had traveled with her from Independence.

"My stepson is married to your stepdaughter. I have a feeling we'll see each other a great deal." Melody looked out over the garden. "I don't know why they thought they'd need so many pumpkins, but this isn't going to be a quick job to harvest them all."

"Fiona just told me that Andrew loves pumpkin pie, so I'm excited to harvest it. Maybe I can put up some pumpkin pie filling to have it for the whole winter ahead."

"I don't know if Jacob enjoys pumpkin pie, but I'd be happy to help," Melody replied. "I saw you at the boarding house on Sunday evening."

"You should have come over and said hello!" Doris said. "We eat there every evening. You'll have to come as our guests one week." She briefly explained their arrangement for free meals to Melody.

"Oh, that sounds fun. The four of us should go sometime soon."

They spent much of the afternoon picking squash and pumpkins. When it was almost five, and time for Doris and Andrew to go to the boarding house for their supper, Fiona drove Doris and eight large pumpkins home. "Your father will want all of this made into pies?" Doris asked. "I do enjoy making pumpkin bread."

"He loves pumpkin bread as well. I wouldn't serve him just pumpkin, but bread and pies would thrill him."

"I'll do that then. I won't even offer to make extra for the store or the boarding house."

"I don't know how you manage to make all you do for them. I stay busy just being a wife and having my garden."

Doris nodded. "Next summer I'll have a garden, and I'll keep busier. Right now, I don't feel like I'm doing much of anything."

"How many loaves of bread do you bake for the store and the boarding house every day?" Fiona asked.

"Just twenty, and then one for your father and me. I churn the butter while the bread is baking, and then I still have a whole day ahead of me. I was going to spend the afternoon sewing the curtains I cut out this morning, but I'm glad I got to help with your harvest instead." Doris planned to give some of the pumpkin pie filling she put up to Fiona to thank her for the help with the harvest.

"There are some wild berries growing out near the lake," Fiona said. "I've been wanting to drive out and pick them, but it's a long drive, and Henri can't go so Emma won't go. I don't want to go alone."

"Why don't you take Melody?" Doris asked, though why she was unsure. She loved the idea of picking berries down by the lake.

Fiona shrugged. "She wants to be there when Henri's baby is born. I do too, but...I want to pick berries while they're ripe as well."

Doris smiled. "I'll pack your father a lunch to take with him tomorrow, and we'll go to the lake and pick all the berries we can find. Jams and jellies and pies...Oh, I do love berries!"

"Wonderful! I'll come to fetch you around seven?"

"Sounds good. I'll pack us a lunch to share when I pack your Pa's lunch for work."

"Thank you!" Fiona said, looking excited at the prospect of spending the day picking berries.

"I'll need to be home by around five," Doris said. "That's when your pa and I go to the boarding house for supper."

"I don't know why you don't just cook at home. I know you're a good cook because Pa told me."

"He likes to go to the boarding house, and I have to admit that Margaret is a better cook than me."

"Pa has spent his whole life saving every dime he can, and now he pays to eat somewhere twice per day."

"Your pa doesn't look at it as paying when he does it all in trade," Doris said, shaking her head. "But if he's happy going there every day, then I'm happy to go with him."

"You're a very good wife to him. I'm glad you came through."

"I try really hard to be a good wife," Doris responded, not willing to say anything about the friction between herself and Fiona's father.

Fiona pulled the wagon into the yard. "Tomorrow at seven!" she reminded her stepmother.

"I'll be ready!" Doris said. They were always home from breakfast by seven. She'd simply make sure to have lunches packed before they went to the boarding house.

Fiona helped her carry the pumpkins inside and put them on the counter before she rushed off to make supper for her own husband. Doris didn't need to make supper, so she waited for Andrew to be finished in the parlor, where she kept working on the curtains she'd started.

When Andrew came in, he looked exhausted. "Are you sure you don't want me to fix something here?" she asked.

He shook his head. "No, we'll go."

"Are you feeling all right?" Doris asked as she followed Andrew to the wagon.

"I'm fine. Just got too hot today. It happens even this far north."

"It'll cool off soon," Doris said. Her favorite thing about Clover Creek so far is it could get very hot during the day in the summer, but it always cooled down at night.

When they reached the boarding house, Doris was excited to see what Margaret had fixed for supper, and to her surprise, it was venison stew. It was all Doris could do not to jump for joy.

"I didn't think you'd ever make this!" Doris said. She'd been close to sending Andrew out hunting for a deer, so she could make it.

It was just as good as she'd imagined, and she sighed as she took the first bite. When she looked up she saw that Andrew was watching her. "Sorry, this is just one of my favorite foods, and I haven't had it since I was a child."

He smiled. "That didn't make sense when you first said it, but now that I know you didn't marry, it does. I'm glad you like it so much."

"I could truly eat this for every meal. I'm going to be as round as a ball if we keep eating here twice per day," she said, though she'd never really had any problems with her weight.

He shrugged. "I won't mind."

For the first time, Doris asked for more food at the boarding house that night. "I could take gallons of this home and never be satisfied," she told Margaret.

"Glad to hear you say that," Margaret said. When she came back with the bowl of stew, her husband was behind her with a large jar filled with the stew. "This is for all you do for us."

Doris held back the squeal that wanted to come out. "Thank you so much!"

"You're welcome." Margaret disappeared to help her other guests, while Doris dug into the next bowl of stew.

"I'll serve this for lunch the day after tomorrow," Doris said.

Andrew frowned. "Not tomorrow?"

"Oh! I forgot to tell you. Fiona and I are going to the lake tomorrow to pick berries."

"I see." Somehow he didn't seem thrilled she was going to spend the day with his daughter.

"Is that all right?" she asked, surprised.

"I've gotten used to having lunch with you at the house every day," he said softly.

"I'll make you a lunch. But if I can pick berries, we can have jams and pies for the winter."

He nodded. "I know."

Doris was astonished. He was going to miss her. It was the first indication he'd given that he really enjoyed spending time with her. Maybe it was good she wouldn't be home all day for a change. "Do you want me to cancel?"

Andrew shook his head. "No, that's all right. I do like the idea of having some berry pies this winter."

"I helped pick pumpkins all day," she said softly. "I'll be putting up pumpkin pie filling by the end of the week, and I thought I could make some pumpkin bread…"

He grinned. "You can spend time with Fiona any time you'd like."

Chapter Seven

The next day was great fun for Doris. She'd worked hard her entire life, and it felt good to be outside working again. Fiona was feeling chatty, and she talked about her mother some while Doris took mental notes of everything said.

"I'm sure you miss her terribly," Doris said.

"Oh, I do. I wasn't sure she'd make the journey all the way to Oregon City and back to here, but she did. And then she died when we were settled here. I can't imagine anything harder than losing my mother."

"The two of you were close?"

"Oh, yes. We were close before the Trail, but after walking that far with her, and having her as my closest companion, it was so much harder to lose her. When she and Pa fell ill last winter, I worried I'd lose them both, but Pa pulled through. I did all the milking for two weeks, but it was enough for him to get better. The day he went back to work is the day we lost Ma. I blamed myself for a while, and I know Pa blamed himself for not being there, but she was so sick, and she was so tired. I think it was a blessing that she died when she did."

"She wasn't unhappy, was she?" The little Doris had heard about Nelita had always been positive. It was hard to believe she hadn't been happy.

"Oh, yes, she was happy! We worked so hard to prepare for the winter, so we'd have the food we needed, and Pa promised her a new house this summer. She got weaker the further west we came." Fiona shook her head. "It still seems so strange to me that she's gone, but I know those last six months, she was barely hanging on. She worked hard, despite how she was feeling."

"She sounds like she was a perfect wife and mother."

"No one's perfect," Fiona said. "She had a bit of a temper and would get angry when I didn't learn to do something properly the first time. And she got frustrated with Pa. Always called him a skinflint. Far from perfect, but she was the Ma I needed to grow into the person I am today."

"She and your pa were happy together?" Doris asked.

"Oh, they were. Pa would bring her special rocks he found while he was out during the day. He always wanted to farm, but where we lived back east, he worked in a factory. He's a lot happier here, even without Ma."

"Did you ever lie to your parents growing up?"

Fiona shook her head. "Not after the first time. Pa was so angry with me, I'm surprised I can sit down today. Lying is not something he'll ever tolerate."

Doris felt worse than ever. It sounded like she'd done the absolute worst thing she could have done in her husband's eyes. "You must miss living with them."

"In some ways I do," Fiona said. "But I love the freedom I have as a wife. Sam is very soft spoken, and if I tell him it will help us for me to do something, then he's always happy for me to do it. It's funny sometimes just how much he agrees with me. I don't take advantage of him, but I could if I wanted to."

"I'm glad you don't take advantage of him," Doris said as she dropped a few more of the berries into her basket. "What kind of berries are these anyway?"

"They're a form of huckleberry, but I'm not sure which. I know they're safe to eat, but they tend to be very bitter. They need lots of sugar to make them taste good."

"Well, we'll see what kind of pie they make. Or jam. Or both. The berries are so small it seems to be taking forever to pick a decent amount of them."

"It does," Fiona agreed. "I think it would be better if we could mix them with other berries, but all of the wild ones except these were ripe earlier in the season. The gooseberries here are wonderful. I have several jars of gooseberry jam at home."

"That sounds good."

"Oh, you have some in your cellar that I picked for Pa last month. I'm sure he hasn't eaten it all. He probably hasn't had any. I worked hard to keep his cellar stocked with food, but he never really cared to touch it." Fiona shook her head. "He lost his appetite after Ma died. I'm glad to see he's gaining back a little of the weight he lost now that he's married to you."

"I hadn't noticed. I hope I'm helping him gain his weight back. I know he prefers to eat at the boarding house for most meals. I am a good cook though. I swear I am!"

Fiona laughed. "He said you were. I think he's just set in his ways, and he wants to do things the way he has since I married. It seems to give him comfort to have the same routine all the time."

"That makes sense. He does seem to be a creature of habit. I'm surprised he was willing to travel the Oregon Trail where everything would be different."

"I was too in some ways, but I don't think he thought of the trail as a big change in his life. He's always dreamed of working for himself as a dairy farmer, and it was the only way he could see to fulfilling his dream."

"I think that makes sense." Doris wasn't sure if that would have worked for her, but she wasn't the one who had problems with change.

"You just have to look past his eccentricities to the good man he is under them all," Fiona said with a grin. "I am glad you two married. I think it'll be good for both of you."

"It certainly has been for me," Doris said.

On the long drive back to town, Doris asked more personal questions about Andrew. "What's your pa's favorite food?"

Fiona shrugged. "Pa is easy. As long as he has meat and potatoes, he's a happy man."

"You said he doesn't like squash," Doris said.

"Yes, he likes meat, potatoes, bread, and desserts. He will pick vegetables out of soups, and if you're looking for a vegetable he'll eat, it's better to just give up."

Doris smiled. "My pa was the same way."

"Then it shouldn't be hard for you to cook for Pa. I'm sure he's thrilled with whatever you do though. He seems to be very fond of you."

Fond. Yes, he did seem to be fond of her. But she wanted him to love her. She hoped she hadn't already messed her marriage up where love could never happen.

She was home just in time to go to supper with Andrew, and he had already hitched the wagon when she and Fiona pulled into the yard. Fiona waved her on. "Go to supper. I'll put the berries in the kitchen for when you're ready."

"Thank you." Surprising herself, Doris embraced the girl. "You have no idea how much help you've given me today. Thank you!"

Fiona grinned. "I was happy to have someone willing to go berry picking with me."

Doris got into the wagon with Andrew. He glanced at her. "Looks like you got a little burned by the sun," he said, nodding to her face. "Didn't you wear your bonnet?"

She laughed. "I kept taking it off because it made me hot. I guess I did that one time too many and got too much sun."

"It would seem so." He shook his head. "You're a great deal like Fiona. Always ready for your next adventure."

"Is that a bad thing?" she asked.

"No, I don't think so. It just surprises me because you seem so hard-working."

"If you don't think picking huckleberries all day is hard work, then you don't know what hard work is. And then I'll take the berries and make jam out of them. Women's work is different from men's work, but it's still hard work."

Andrew nodded. "I suppose you're right."

"I'm always willing to help with the milking or any other farm task," she said. "You just have to let me know."

"I appreciate that," he said. He still spoke a lot less than he had before she'd admitted her deceit to him.

After supper, he took the long way home, pointing out different places in town, including the doctor's office and the blacksmith shop. He showed her where the Kings had their furniture business. "It's a good town. I can't imagine that I would have been as comfortable anywhere else."

"I'm glad this is where you ended up then. Was your wife happy here?" she asked.

He looked at her for a moment. "Nelita? Sure, she was happy here. Anywhere with Fiona and I would have made her happy. I wish she'd lived long enough to see Fiona married. That would have truly made her happy."

"I'm really sorry you lost her."

"Thank you. She was my wife for twenty years. My life would have been very different without her by my side."

Finally, he pulled into their yard. "Get your dough mixed for tomorrow," he said. "I'm going to work on something in the barn for a bit."

"What are you working on?" she asked, wondering if he'd be willing to tell her.

"Nothing much," he said.

Doris went into the house wondering why he was keeping secrets from her. Was it because she'd deceived him unintentionally? She wished there was some way for her to make amends and for him to start trusting her again.

She went inside and got the dough mixed and taken to the cellar. When she came back up the stairs, she could hear him walking through the house. "Andrew?" she called, wondering where she could find him.

"In here!" he called.

She followed his voice to his bedroom where he was getting ready for bed. "I'm tired too," she told him. "I haven't spent that much time outside since I got to Clover Creek."

He smiled, reaching out for her. "Are you too tired?"

She chuckled. "I enjoy what we do too much to be too tired."

"Good," he said, lowering his mouth to hers. Not much was said for a long while after.

The next two days were spent making and putting up jam, and putting up the pumpkin pie filling. To surprise Andrew, Doris baked a loaf of pumpkin bread for him, hoping he'd be as happy as Fiona had thought he would be.

She served the bread as part of their lunch on Friday, and at first, Andrew poked at it with his knife instead of buttering it. "What's in it?" he finally asked.

"It's pumpkin bread," she said. "You'll love it."

He looked skeptical as he buttered the sliver of a piece he'd cut for himself. She could see he was only eating it so he wouldn't hurt her feelings, which she couldn't complain about one whit.

He took a bite of the bread and his whole face lit up. "This is delicious!"

Doris smiled, thrilled he liked it. "I'm glad you like it! I packed a few pieces in your oilcloth bag so you can take it for a snack this afternoon."

"Why do you do such wonderful things for me?" he asked.

She shrugged. "I thought you'd like it so I made it."

"I'm surprised you're being so kind when I know you are worried about the future of our marriage."

Doris swallowed hard, trying to find the right words. "As long as I am your wife, I will make you as happy as I can. If you decide to send me on with the next wagon train, I'll go without complaint." And it was true. Though she had few things that she would need, her wagon was still parked next to camp. She could jump in it and leave any time she wanted to. Or whenever he told her to as the case may be.

"Do you want to leave?" he asked.

Doris shook her head. "I'm happy as your wife, and I want to do as much for you as I can. I hope someday, you will be proud to call me your wife instead of always so disappointed."

He sighed. "I'm not disappointed in you, Doris. I want you to understand that I care for you deeply. I am just having a hard time getting past the lie."

"Do you want to send me away?" she asked.

He shook his head. "No, I don't. I would never get a divorce. But...I can't fully trust you yet either. It's something we're going to have to work through together."

Doris nodded. "I understand." And she did to some extent. But if she'd found out something he'd lied about, she never would have held it against him this way. She'd have found a way to keep loving and trusting him.

When the word love came into her mind, she wanted to reject it, but she couldn't because she knew it was true. She was in love with Andrew Jefferson, even though he couldn't trust her. Maybe someday he'd be able to.

When he left that afternoon to head back to work, she washed the dishes, and then went to work on the curtains she'd started. She wanted curtains and a tablecloth to match. It would make her feel so much more at home, and she said a silent prayer it would make him feel at home as well. She wanted his love and respect, and she wasn't sure she'd ever get it.

While Andrew worked that afternoon, his mind was constantly on Doris. Yes, she'd lied to him, but she'd told him as soon as she could. And she was a good wife, helping him to make money and feeding him things she knew he'd find special.

He wasn't sure he'd ever be able to trust her completely, but he felt like he'd done the right thing by marrying her. He was happier with her around. He wasn't ready to go so far as to say he loved her yet, and he wouldn't until he trusted her completely. Hopefully that would be very soon.

She was a hard worker, and that was obvious. She didn't have a great deal to do around the house since they ate out two meals per day, so she worked for others to occupy her time.

And she was very willing and ready in bed. Oh, how he'd missed that special part of his relationship with Nelita. Doris was slowly taking his late wife's place. It was time for him to start trusting her if at all possible. He prayed that it would come quickly because she was the woman he needed in his life.

Chapter Eight

By the first of October, the harvest was done, and all of the vegetables had been put up, ready to use when Doris needed them.

But that gave her even less to do on a daily basis. In her spare time, she started quilting. She had no one to make a quilt for, but she wanted to sleep under a quilt made by her own hands and not by Nelita.

So she did all her chores in the morning and in the afternoons, she worked on quilting. The puppy, whom she'd decided to name Storm, still wasn't quite ready to join her in the house, so she visited him in the mornings as well, hoping that he would understand that she was his human.

She talked to Fiona who told her that Andrew's favorite color was blue, and he liked red a lot as well. So she bought yards of red and blue fabric and started to create the quilt she wanted them to sleep under.

On Wednesday afternoons, she went to the quilting circle at the church and got to know many of the women in a way she couldn't before and after church services. She felt herself especially drawn to Mrs. Mitchell, the midwife who had once called the Oregon Trail a death march.

She had many children of her own, and they were close to the same age. Doris respected the other woman as she talked of her family and how she'd given up everything to come west to follow a dream her husband had, but she'd never shared.

Mrs. Mitchell was a new grandmother, sometimes having the baby with her at the quilting circle because her daughter, Mary, had gone off hunting.

"Does your daughter hunt often?" Doris asked as she carefully stitched.

Mrs. Mitchell nodded. "She was my only for several years, and her father took her out hunting, fishing, and doing whatever he thought was fun. She's more comfortable with a musket than she is with a pot, but I made sure she could cook as well. And she's always had to help mind her younger siblings. Mary's a good daughter, but she outshoots her husband, and he seems to respect her for it."

Doris laughed. "She sounds very interesting. I'm sorry I haven't had time to get to know her yet."

"She is definitely interesting." Mrs. Mitchell looked down at the beautiful little girl she was holding. "I'm a little afraid she's going to raise this little angel to be just like her mother, but I'll love her no matter what."

Hannah, the pastor's wife, moved over to sit near them. She tried to spend at least a little time talking to everyone in the quilting circle every week. "Are you talking about Mary?" Hannah asked, smiling.

"I am," Mrs. Mitchell said. "She tried to turn you into a musket-carrying woman as well."

"She did try, and I'm so thankful to her that I know how to shoot a musket and do so many other things that aren't exactly womanly. I don't think she changed me in any way."

"Oh, you were a good girl to begin with. Not like my Mary." Mrs. Mitchell shook her head.

Hannah laughed delightedly. "I love your daughter and consider her one of my very closest friends."

"I know."

It was the most Doris had ever heard the preacher's wife say, and she was happy to get to know her a little better. "Did you come west with everyone else?"

Hannah nodded. "My stepfather all but sold me to Jed, and I was very unhappy at first, but it didn't take long for me to realize what a truly good man I'd married, and I was very happy to be his wife."

"That's wonderful," Doris said.

"What about your first husband?" Hannah asked.

Doris spent a moment contemplating what she should say, and she finally said, "I've never been married before. I pretended to be a widow to keep unwanted attentions away on the trail. I never meant to continue the lie here, and I must say, I'm incredibly sorry that anyone ever believed I was married before."

Hannah smiled, nodding. "I understand completely. Many of the women in this room have pasts they're not proud of."

"So you don't think less of me?" Doris asked, surprised the preacher's wife would be so casual about such a big lie.

"Of course not. I'm assuming you've told Mr. Jefferson the truth?" At Doris's nod, Hannah continued. "As far as I'm concerned it's between the two of you and no one else's business. If you two can work it out, then all is good in the world."

"I've never met a preacher's wife who found it so easy to forgive someone for lying the way I did."

"I don't think I'm like most preacher's wives. At least I hope I'm not. I just try to be open-minded and understand people and where they're coming from. And I support my husband with everything inside me."

"That's wonderful. I'm trying to do the same."

"I've heard about the baking you're doing to help Margaret. I don't know how she's going to manage in another month when that baby is born," Mrs. Mitchell said, changing the subject.

"I don't either." Doris shook her head. "I do what I can to help, but it won't be enough."

"Oh, it will," Hannah said. "Many of us are already discussing which day we'll take over for her."

Fiona, who was behind Doris, said, "I'm taking Mondays and Thursdays. I think it'll be good for me to be out of the house two days a week. Then I can forget about my morning sickness."

It was the first Doris had heard about morning sickness. "Are you expecting?" she asked excitedly. At Fiona's nod, she continued, "Oh, I've always wanted to be a grandmother. I do hope you'll let me help with the baby."

Fiona smiled. "Of course. I haven't told Pa yet, but I plan to when we all go to supper on Sunday evening."

"He's going to be so excited," Doris said. She knew her husband loved being a father, and she couldn't imagine how happy he'd be to be a grandfather.

Fiona laughed. "Just don't tell him yet!"

"I wouldn't." Doris's mind returned to Margaret. "Do you think she'd let me take a day cooking? I'd be happy to help her."

"I think she'd be thrilled," Fiona said. "I know Hannah is taking a day, I'm taking two, Trudie will take a day, and with you, that's five days covered. She'll only have to find two more people to help."

"I'd even take two days if it would help more," Doris said. "I love to cook, and I only get to cook lunches because Andrew loves going to the boarding house so much."

"Oh, then she'd only have one day left to fill. I think Emma would be happy to take that last day, and then she wouldn't have to worry as she took a few weeks off to be with her children and recover from childbirth. I can't wait to tell her!"

Margaret was across the circle. As much as she worked, she tried to make it to the quilting circle every week.

Fiona looked across the quilt to the other side of the room. "Margaret!"

Margaret turned with a sweet smile. "Yes?"

"Doris is going to take two days, and I'm going to talk Emma into taking one. That will fill your week."

Margaret looked confused for a moment, and then her eyes widened. "Oh, that would be wonderful! Are you sure you don't mind?" she asked Doris.

"Not at all. I love to cook, and you're so good at it that I never get a chance."

Margaret laughed softly. "I'm very happy for the help."

When Fiona drove Doris home that afternoon, Doris was excited to tell Andrew what she'd agreed to. He may not like it, but he would definitely understand she wanted to help others.

On their way to supper that evening, Doris sat close beside Andrew, drinking in his warmth. "I'm going to work at the boarding house for two days per week while Margaret is recovering from childbirth," she told him.

"Really? Are you getting paid?" he asked.

"I don't think so. And I wouldn't accept it if she offered. I just want it to be my gift to her and the baby."

Andrew smiled. "You are a very giving woman, Doris."

"I try to do things to help others that I know they need. I've already crocheted a blanket for the baby." She so wanted to tell him that he was going to be a grandfather, but she wouldn't betray Fiona's trust that way. "Since I'm too old to have babies, I think I'll just help everyone in town who has one. Then I can hold babies and feel like I've had time with children."

He smiled and nodded. "My Nelita did that as well. She always wanted a dozen children, but we were only able to have Fiona."

"I'm sorry," Doris said, understanding completely. "I never thought I'd be a spinster until I was forty-five. I always dreamed of having a big family."

"Do others in town know you were a spinster?"

"I just told Hannah Scott today. Well, she and Mrs. Mitchell, and I'm pretty certain Fiona heard as well. I think it's time I came clean with everyone."

"I think so as well," he said smiling at her. "Thank you for telling people."

"No problem. I never meant for the lie to follow me in my new life. It was just to keep me safe on the trail."

"I can understand that," he said softly. And all at once, he did understand her reason for lying. He definitely didn't want to hear another lie cross her lips, but he knew he needed to trust her again. Truthfully, she'd done nothing so terribly wrong that he should worry.

Margaret looked both exhausted and happy when she came to their table with their glasses of milk. "Thank you for agreeing to help with the boarding house while I'm out with the baby. I'm having everyone come one day next week so I can show them how I do things."

"I'll be here."

"I can't pay more than twenty-five cents per day. Will that be all right?"

"No," Doris said. "I won't take anything from you. I'm just happy to help."

"Oh, I couldn't ask you to do that!"

"You're not asking. I'm telling you that's what I'm doing. It's my way of saying thank you for being my first friend in Clover Creek."

Margaret had tears in her eyes as she hurried off to get their suppers for them.

"You're a good woman, Doris Jefferson," Andrew said. "I don't think I realized just how good you are until today."

"I'm doing what I would want someone to do for me," Doris responded. "There are so many babies being born here, and I want to do what I can to help each and every new mother."

He reached across the table and covered her hand with his. "I'm proud to call you my wife."

As he hadn't touched her in public since she'd confessed her lie to him, she was thrilled that he was holding her hand now. "I'm proud to call you my husband." For the first time since she had told him, it felt as if their marriage could actually work in a way that they would both be happy for the rest of their lives.

She looked down at the table, fearing he would see the tears that had popped into her eyes. She didn't want him to see her cry. She only wanted him to love her as much as she loved him.

On the drive home that night, he held her close, and after she'd finished her baking that evening, they made love. While they made love often, this time it felt as if he'd truly forgiven her for her wrongdoing. It was different, and so was he.

As they snuggled together to sleep, Doris realized that she was the luckiest woman in the world. Her husband had forgiven her, and she was going to rejoice that he had for the rest of her life.

One lie had caused her so much grief that she promised herself she would never lie again, even if it meant being protected from anything. No, she would be truthful every day for the rest of her life.

By Sunday, Doris was so excited for Andrew to find out about the baby, she could barely contain herself. At church, she was thinking about the baby as she whispered to Fiona she had to tell her father soon. "I'm going to explode if he doesn't find out."

Fiona laughed. "I'm telling him tonight. I sure hope he just feels happy when I tell him and not old. My father is not an old man."

"No, he's not," Doris agreed thinking of the way the man made love to her. He was anything but old.

They all sat in the parlor before going to supper that evening, when Fiona, interrupted the men's talk about weather. Why did men always seem to feel the need to talk about weather, and what it may bring, when there was nothing they could do about it?

"Pa?" Fiona said.

Andrew turned from his conversation with Sam. "Yes?"

"You're going to be a grandpa in the spring."

Andrew stared at his daughter for a moment before a slow smile spread across his face. "I can't wait to hold my grandbaby."

Sam grinned. "I've been waiting for her to tell you. We were hoping you'd make the cradle."

"I would happily make the cradle!" Andrew said. "You don't want to?"

Sam shook his head. "I could, but it would mean so much more to Fiona if you did it."

Andrew smiled as he looked at his daughter and son-in-law. They were making him a grandfather. And he loved and trusted his sweet wife more than he could express. His life, which had felt as if it was ending just nine months before, felt as if it was the most wonderful life on earth. Between Doris and Fiona, he was as happy as a clam.

Doris grinned. "I know I'm not your real mother, but I will be the best grandma I can possibly be. I even started a crocheted blanket for the baby."

Andrew looked at his wife. "You knew and didn't tell me?" he was surprised she could keep a secret of that magnitude.

"I promised her I wouldn't on Wednesday when she told me. I don't think I could have kept it in for much longer though. We're going to be grandparents!" Doris couldn't have been more excited if it had been a natural grandchild. She would have a baby to love, and that's all she had ever truly wanted.

Chapter Nine

By the time Margaret had her baby a few weeks later, Doris was feeling more settled in her marriage with Andrew. Sure, he'd never said he trusted her, but he acted as if he did. And though the word love was never spoken, she fell more in love with him daily. She only hoped his feelings were the same.

Working at the boarding house two days per week meant getting up even earlier than she had been. Getting up at three in the morning felt ridiculous, but she would do what she could to help her friend.

Margaret had given birth to a boy, and they'd named him Alexander, which was quickly shortened to Alex. On a Friday morning in late November, Margaret brought her son to the boarding house with her, planning to visit with Doris on her last day of cooking all the meals for the boarding house.

"He's beautiful," Doris said.

Margaret smiled. "We certainly think so." Her girls were sitting quietly at the table, drawing pictures.

Margaret had provided the menus for the time she would be out, and that morning, Doris was making scrambled eggs, biscuits, and gravy. While she talked to Margaret, she was cooking enough food for the thirty people they would have for breakfast.

The boarding house hadn't opened for breakfast yet, but it would in just a few minutes. Doris had enjoyed working there, but she was pleased she was almost finished. She wanted to start making the Christmas gift she'd chosen for Andrew. And there were so many things she wanted to make for Fiona's baby.

As she fixed the plates for the first of the boarders, Doris listened to Margaret talk about the baby. "He has the best temperament. I think he's going to do fine lying in a cradle here in the kitchen while I work."

"It sounds like you've figured everything out," Doris responded. "Give me a moment to get these first plates out." She balanced four plates on her arms and hurried out of the kitchen, distributing the plates where she could, and then she hurried back for the coffee pot and walked around filling coffee cups.

Back in the kitchen, she started on the second batch of eggs. The biscuits were made, and there was enough gravy for the entire meal. It was just making sure she always made fresh eggs.

For the rest of the day, Doris was in and out of the kitchen, being both the cook and the waitress. She'd gotten to know so many of the people in town by working for Margaret that she already felt as if she was one of Clover Creek inhabitants.

Margaret watched her girls and fed the baby on and off during the two-hour breakfast shift. "You act as if you've done this all your life," Margaret said, admiring Doris.

"I've cooked all my life. I haven't cooked in this volume or ever served so many people, but it seems to come naturally."

"Just don't open a restaurant," Margaret joked. "I don't need the competition."

"I wouldn't be competition for you," Doris responded. "Everyone in town is still asking when you'll be back. I feel as if I'm falling short every day."

"That's not true! They want me back because they're used to me."

Doris knew better, but she felt no need to argue with her friend. "Supper today is roast beef, mashed potatoes with gravy, and carrots. I'll serve fresh bread and butter with it."

Margaret smiled. "Everyone loves roast beef night. I'm thankful for all the help you've given me. Are you sure I can't pay you for all the work you've done?"

Doris shook her head. "No, you can't. Working for you has helped me to get to know people in town, and I've learned how to cook for much larger groups of people. Skills that must be useful in the future. Especially if Fiona has the dozen children she told me she wanted."

Margaret laughed and shook her head. "I would never turn down a blessing from God in the form of a child, but a dozen feels like a few too many. My three will be hard enough to juggle."

Doris nodded, hurrying out of the kitchen to serve more plates of food and top up people's coffee. She'd been washing dishes as they returned, so she was almost done for the morning."

"Would you mind if I tried to do supper on my own tonight?" Margaret asked. "I want to see if I'm ready to work again, and I'm itching to get behind that huge stove and cook."

"I wouldn't mind at all!" Doris said. "I wouldn't mind coming here and working with you tonight as well."

"No, I want to try to do it on my own."

"All right. We'll be here at five as we are every evening. If you need help, just let me know, and I'll be here."

Margaret smiled. "Andrew must be thrilled to have a wife who is so willing to give of herself."

Doris just smiled at that. There were no words to express how complicated her marriage had become.

After breakfast, Doris hurried out to Andrew who had been waiting for her. She had eaten her own breakfast in the kitchen in between all the work she had to do. It seemed to work well.

"Margaret is going to do the supper service on her own tonight," Doris said as she pulled on her coat. She thinks she's ready."

Andrew smiled. "So I get my wife back?"

Doris laughed. "I think I managed to take care of both you and the boarding house."

"Oh, you did. I just like knowing you're at home while I'm out on the farm." He put his arm around her as they walked out to the wagon. "So what will you do with all your spare time?"

"I'm working on so many different sewing projects that I will not be bored if that's what you're asking. Fiona asked for help with the baby's clothes." And she was almost finished with the quilt she was making for their bed. She was certain Andrew had noticed it, but he'd yet to say a word.

On the drive back to the farm, Doris thought about all the things she should do that day. Now that she had most of it free. "Do you mind having leftover stew from yesterday for lunch?"

"I never mind. It's always so much better than the jerky I took out for myself. I'm going to do some hunting today. Most of my projects for fair weather are done for the year, and the cows are in the barn. There's no need for me to keep trying to find things to do. Hopefully, I'll have some game for you to put up tomorrow."

Doris nodded. "That would be nice." She was still thinking about venison stew. As good as Margaret's had been, Doris wanted the venison stew she remembered. "Try for a deer."

He chuckled. "If I get a deer, will I eat venison stew for a solid week?"

"More like a month," Doris said, teasing him.

"It's a good thing I like venison stew then, isn't it?"

"I'll serve it with biscuits," she said, trying to entice him.

"I'll get a deer if I can. I'd never had elk before coming here, but elk jerky became one of my favorite things. Mrs. Williams will let me take her an elk, she'll process it, and take ten percent of the jerky for her family as payment. I don't know what she does differently than everyone else in town, but her jerky is more tender and more flavorful than any other."

"It sounds like she's a wonderful cook," Doris said. She wasn't very good at making jerky herself.

Andrew laughed. "Worst cook in town. The only thing she makes well is jerky, but she's very good at making jerky."

"Huh." Doris was surprised. "Let's have her do it then. I'm not good at it myself. I'd never even attempted to make jerky before the trail, and then I never felt like I got it just right."

"I think that's perfect. And we're helping others at the same time because we're giving them food for the winter."

"I'm glad we both agree that helping others is important," Doris said. "Many people don't even think to help."

"It's important in a community like this. It helps people to be able to trade. Margaret couldn't make a profit if she had to pay for the bread, milk, and butter. Same with the store. But when we offer a trade, making a profit becomes easier for them."

"And it helps us as well." She'd never really thought about trading services as being helpful to both people before. She thought it was just because Andrew kept his purse strings tighter than most.

"Exactly. I wouldn't be willing to eat at the boarding house fourteen meals a week if I was paying. They charge fifteen cents a meal! But since I trade with milk, it works out beautifully. The only way I make real money is with the dairy, but I need little because of the way I trade for everything. Even the lumber in this house was traded for. I gave them milk, and they gave me lumber. I'm still paying off the lumber with milk, but they have said a bottle a day for five years would be enough. I can do that!"

"It sounds like everyone in town does pitch together to make things happen."

"We got used to helping each other on the trail. And now that we're a community instead of a company, Pastor Jed encourages us to always help others. At this time last year, he gave a sermon I'll never forget. He told us to look around the congregation and find someone with a need. They didn't have to ask, or say they had a need. It was our responsibility to find them. And then help them fill that need."

"I like that!" Doris had never heard of a preacher doing that, but she loved it.

"It worked very well. My family and I adopted a young widow and her four children. We made them supper every day for the winter. Fiona delivered them all. She also spent one afternoon a week in their home minding the children so the mother could have time with friends. We'll have to pick a family this year."

"Has that woman remarried?" Doris asked.

"Not that I know of," Andrew responded. "She was able to grow a garden this year, and her oldest son was out hunting a lot. I'm not sure they need anything, but I'd be happy to ask."

"Do that. I'd be more than happy to help her if she needed it." And then her mind drifted to others. There were so many in the community with needs. "Perhaps you can shoot two elk, and we can share half the jerky we get with others who are short of food."

"Perfect. And that helps the Williams even more." He stopped the wagon in front of the house. "I'm going to unhitch the wagon and see what I can get today. I've never been much of a hunter, but living here, you need to be."

"Wouldn't it be easier if you hunted with a friend? That way you wouldn't have to carry the animal back here on your own."

"Not a bad idea. I'll go see if Sam is free."

Watching Andrew drive off for a moment, Doris couldn't believe how much she loved the man. She couldn't imagine her life without him after a short three months of marriage. He was a good man through and through.

In the house, she put the leftover stew on one corner of the stove to heat slowly, and she brought the shirt she was making him into the kitchen to finish the hemming. She'd noticed his shirts were wearing out, and she loved sewing so much. It just made sense to her to make him shirts for Christmas. Well, shirts and the quilt that would cover them.

Then she realized that was a way she could help others. She could sew shirts in different sizes and gift them to men who were wearing worn shirts but had no family to make them. The store sold no premade clothes, so there was a definite need in the community.

She hid the shirt as soon as it was finished. She'd wrap it in brown paper and put it out for him for Christmas.

By lunchtime, she'd done some more of the quilting, and she was pleased with the progress there. Soon, they would sleep under a quilt she had made instead of the one he'd shared with Nelita. As much as he cared for his first wife, he had to understand that his second wife needed things around that she'd done and could be proud of.

Both Sam and Andrew were there for lunch. "We got an elk," Andrew said, beaming with pride. "I shot it, but I never would have gotten it down the mountain without Sam."

"That's wonderful," Doris said as she set another place at the table for Sam. "Just one more elk and some venison for today then."

Sam laughed. "You're expecting a lot of us."

"There is a lot of wildlife here," Doris countered. "It shouldn't be a problem for the two of you." She sat down to enjoy the meal with them. "Will you take the elk straight to Mrs. Williams?"

"After lunch, we will," Andrew said. "I can't wait to eat that jerky."

Sam nodded. "Mrs. Williams makes the best jerky around. Don't eat anything else she tries to give you."

Doris thought then it might be a nice gesture to take some meals to the Williams family. They must not be eating well. "What does the family eat?" she asked.

"Oh, they have meals. They just don't taste good. She burns everything. Henri has given the girls of the family cooking lessons, and they try to cook every meal now, but sometimes Mrs. Williams insists." Sam shook his head. "They're wonderful people, but Mrs. Williams can't cook to save her life."

"Except jerky," Doris said.

"Except jerky," Sam agreed. "And no one makes jerky that's half as good as Mrs. Williams. It's like she only has the capacity to cook one thing well, so she's settled on jerky. I'm just glad she's willing to process what we take her into jerky and only keep a small amount for her own family. It makes things so much easier."

"I'm glad her daughters can cook then."

"So are they," Sam said with a grin.

Andrew just grinned. He was proud of himself for getting the elk, but even more proud of his Doris. She was a good cook and a pleasant wife. He couldn't imagine anyone else who could have fit into his established life and completed him so perfectly.

Chapter Ten

Christmas came quickly. Doris had finished two shirts for Andrew, but she had a pile of others, all wrapped in brown paper with the size written on the outside of the package.

On Christmas Eve, they went to church leaving Storm in the barn as he had a habit of destroying things when they weren't home. Doris had all the shirts in the back of the wagon, more than twenty total over a large range of sizes.

At the Christmas Eve service, held after sundown on Christmas Eve, Pastor Jed talked about the birth of Christ, and the sacrifice he made for humanity. And then he talked about giving.

"I'd like to see everyone in this congregation choose a family to give to or help this winter. Do you know of a widow who lives alone? She may need food. If not, she may need companionship. Even if you can't afford to help others in a physical way, could you spend time with those young children who have lost their father? Could you let their mother go out for a few hours one day a week, just so she can get a break from being both father and mother? Everyone here needs something, and most don't have the courage to ask. Or they have too much pride to ask. I'm not asking you to judge them on their pride. I'd like to see everyone helping someone else in any way they can."

After the sermon, they served hot chocolate and cookies that had been made by various ladies in the church. While they enjoyed the fellowship, Doris kept her eyes open for boys and men who could use new shirts.

Andrew went back and forth from the wagon for her a good ten times as she distributed her gifts to people of the Bear Lake Valley, each of them shocked to receive a gift and sorry they had nothing in return.

After all the shirts had been passed out, Pastor Jed walked over to where the Jeffersons stood sipping their hot chocolate. "I've noticed all the gifts you've given out. What was in them?"

Doris smiled. "Just shirts. I realized so many men and boys had no one to sew for them, so I made twenty shirts in different sizes. They're not fancy, but they are clean and new and have no holes."

Jed grinned. "I wish I'd known, so I could have used you as an example in my sermon tonight."

"I'd rather no one said anything," Doris said. "It's just my way of giving back to a community that has made me feel like one of them from the day I arrived."

"I thank you for loving your community so much," Jed said to Doris before turning to Andrew. "I hope you realize what a gem of a wife you've got here."

Doris blushed, looking down. "I don't know about that."

"I do." With that, Pastor Jed moved on to talk to other people.

On the drive home, Andrew cleared his throat. "Pastor Jed is right. I married a virtual stranger because I needed a wife since I couldn't stand the thought of a winter alone with no one beside me. I had no idea what a wonderful person I was marrying. Someone I can trust with everything inside me."

The word trust had Doris in tears. "Do you mean it? You can finally trust me?"

"I've known I could trust you for a long time," he said. "I should have told you, but I didn't want to bring it up. It's all water under the bridge now."

"Thank you."

"No, thank you. I didn't just wake up and decide to trust you one day. Instead, I watched you and the things you do. The way you help others and give of yourself completely. There's no woman in the world I would choose over you," she said.

"Well, other than Nelita," Doris said.

"I loved Nelita with my whole heart and soul," Andrew said softly. "But she's my past, and you're my present and future. You may not have been my first love, but you're my forever love. I love you with everything inside me, Doris."

Doris blinked, trying to stem the flow of tears. "I love you too, Andrew." Never having dreamed those words would be spoken to her, Doris felt as if she was floating on air. "Thank you for accepting me despite my lie."

When they woke on Christmas morning, Doris went into the kitchen to fix breakfast. She didn't think Margaret should have to cook on Christmas Day.

As she walked past the parlor, she saw a huge piece of furniture in it. She walked inside to look and ran her fingers over the beautifully finished wood. It was an armoire, and it was something she desperately needed. All of her dresses would hang beautifully in it.

Andrew walked up behind her. "Merry Christmas," he said as he wrapped his arms around her waist.

"Oh, thank you, Andrew. Merry Christmas to you as well." She turned in his arms and expressed her gratitude with a soft kiss. "I have gifts for you as well."

He nodded. "I know. Let's get our bread baked and I'll get the milk ready so we can go deliver to town."

"I was going to make a special breakfast," she said softly.

"Let's just eat with Margaret like we do every day."

Doris smiled and nodded. He was right. There was no reason for her to do extra work on Christmas. She hurried into the kitchen to put the bread in to bake, happy that at this time of year, there was no need to put it in the cellar. The whole house was cold until the fire was started.

The bread was baked, and the butter was churned before Andrew came inside from milking. He helped her wrap each loaf of bread in cloth, and the two of them headed to town to deliver the milk, bread, and butter.

In the dining room of the boarding house, they realized there were very few people eating that morning. Most had chosen to do other things than make Margaret work. "I'm sorry that you have to work on Christmas!" Doris said as Margaret hurried over to fill their coffee cups.

"I knew what I was getting into when I opened my business," Margaret said with a smile.

Doris handed her friend a package she'd wrapped a few days before.

Margaret turned it over in her hands. Finally, she untied the string and found the new dish cloths Doris had painstakingly sewn for her. "I noticed your others were getting worn out. I thought having a few more would be perfect for the boarding house."

"Thank you!" Margaret smiled sweetly. "You always think of everything."

Hurrying to the kitchen, Margaret came out with their breakfast. "I'll be around to refill coffee," she said as she disappeared again.

"I love my armoire," Doris told Andrew between bites. "I've never owned anything quite so lovely."

"I wish I could say I made it, but I don't have the skills to make something quite so beautiful. I hired Mr. King, our local furniture maker, and I told him what I wanted."

"What did you trade?" she asked.

He shook his head. "I paid full price for once. I didn't even think about trading."

Doris gaped at him for a moment. He'd paid for something, and she'd never seen him do that. He tithed to the church of course, but it was the only time she'd ever seen him part with his money. "I can't believe you did that."

"Why not? I love you. Money is important, yes, and I hope to leave this earth with a good sum for Fiona, but you're more important. You are my wife, and the woman I love. Of course I'm willing to spend money on you."

"You really do love me." Although she hadn't disbelieved him the night before, knowing he'd spent a tidy sum of money on her for Christmas made the truth truly sink in.

"I told you I do! I don't say things like that without meaning them."

"I know...but it didn't strike me until you paid money for something for me."

He chuckled. "There's no reason not to spend a little on someone I love."

Doris knew the armoire had cost more than a little, but she wasn't about to argue. "I can't wait to get home so you can see the presents I made for you!"

When they got home, they brought Storm into the house with them and went straight to the parlor. Doris fetched the presents she'd hidden under a table in there, and handed him three separate parcels.

Looking down, he frowned. "I only got you one thing."

"Trust me, the thing you got me has a much higher value. I made all of these."

Andrew first opened a shirt and smiled happily. "Mine are all falling apart."

"I noticed, which is why I made the shirts for people around town." She'd already passed out baskets of treats she'd made for people which included jerky, cookies, jam, and other sundry things.

He opened the second to find a different color shirt. "Now I have one for everyday and one for church."

"That's what I was thinking when I made them. I will probably continue to make men's shirts as I have been for people in town who need them."

"I think that's a great idea."

"I'm just using some of the credit we have at the store, which is getting to be a lot." Doris wanted it to be clear she wasn't spending actual money on the materials.

"You could use real money if we ran out." Andrew looked down at the third gift in his hands and was surprised at how heavy it was. "You made this as well?"

"I did." She waited as he opened it, hoping he would be as happy to sleep under something that was theirs as she was.

When he unwrapped the quilt he smiled. "We need something warmer for the winter and this is perfect." He reached out and grasped her hand in his. "It's been almost a year since Nelita passed on. I never thought I'd find someone I could have feelings for after she was gone. But here you are. I thank God every day for you and for Fiona taking the initiative to find me a wife." He pulled her to him and onto his lap. "Christmas is special with you here."

"Christmas is always special, but I'm happy if I make any day better for you."

"I wanted to talk to you about the pastor's sermon last night," he said.

It seemed strange to her that he'd pulled her onto his lap to talk about a sermon. "All right."

"One of the widows in town died last night. I heard about it this morning at the boarding house while you were delivering your bread."

"Oh no!"

"She had a daughter who is fourteen, and the girl has no family around here. It's all back east. How would you feel about adopting her? It would only be for a few years, but you would have a child you could call your own."

"I love that idea! Let's go get her!"

"Are you certain?" he asked. "Taking on a child is a huge responsibility. You should take a moment to think about it."

Doris counted to thirty in her head. "There, I took a moment. Let's go get her!"

Andrew laughed. "She's with the Pastor and Hannah right now, but I'm sure they'll be pleased to find someone who wants her."

Out in the wagon, she couldn't get there fast enough. "What's the girl's name?" she asked.

"Honoria. Her mother was widowed on the trail, and she's been sickly since. I'm not at all surprised she passed."

Doris frowned. "I'll make sure she's taken good care of."

"I know you will."

When they got to the church, where the pastor still lived with his wife and child, Doris jumped off the wagon instead of waiting for Andrew to come around and get her. The only thing she'd felt was missing in her life was a child, and now she would have one, thanks to Andrew's kindness.

When they entered the church, things were quiet. The Scotts lived in a small portion of the church, but everyone entered through the sanctuary when they arrived. Andrew called out, "Pastor Scott!"

Jed came hurrying into the room. "Yes?"

"I was told Honoria is with you. Are you trying to find her a home?"

Jed nodded. "We'll keep her until someone is ready to adopt her."

Doris stepped forward. "We're hoping to adopt her."

"Oh, come and meet her then!" Jed seemed surprised to have already found a home for the orphan, but he seemed happy about it.

Doris and Andrew followed Jed into the far part of the church and went into the home where Jed and his family lived. Hannah was holding a girl and patting her back. "I know things will work out for you." She looked up and her eyes met Doris's.

Doris mouthed the words, "We want her," and Hannah's face lit up.

"Honoria, I want you to meet Andrew and Doris Jefferson. They want to adopt you." Hannah's voice was calm as the girl looked at the older couple.

"Why do you want me?" Honoria asked. "I couldn't even keep my mother alive."

"How long did you have to take care of her?" Doris asked, knowing her background would help with the girl.

"Since Pa died on the trail. I grew a garden this year, and I cooked whatever meat anyone was willing to spare. I...I hate that I killed her."

Doris shook her head. "You didn't kill her. She stayed alive as long as she could for you. I took care of my mother from the time I wasn't much older than you until a little more than a year ago when she passed."

"You did?"

"I did. And I'd love to take you in. I'm not sick, and we can be a real family."

Honoria nodded and got to her feet. "Thank you Pastor Jed. Mrs. Scott."

Hannah smiled. "If you need to talk, remember, we're here."

Honoria, through her sadness and guilt, seemed to be genuinely happy she wouldn't spend her life being a burden on the pastor and his wife. "Thank you for taking me in," she said softly as she got into the back of the wagon.

Doris smiled. "I spent all the years I could have been marrying and having a family taking care of my mother. I'm so happy that I'll have a child now, even if she is mostly grown."

Honoria smiled. "You really want me, don't you?"

"I do. With everything inside me. Andrew and I will be the best parents we can possibly be."

Looking over at Andrew, Doris felt that her life was finally complete. Now she had a daughter to help raise and another who was already going to supply grandchildren. Was it possible for life to get better?

Taking Andrew's hand, Doris said a silent prayer, thanking God for putting Andrew and now Honoria into her life. The words could never be enough though. She was in love and raising a daughter. Life couldn't be more perfect.

www.ingramcontent.com/pod-product-compliance
Lightning Source LLC
LaVergne TN
LVHW092336171025
823772LV00034B/324